NO.1 DAD
IN TEXAS

BY
DIANNE DRAKE

MILLS & BOON

First published in Great Britain 2012
by Mills & Boon, an imprint of Harlequin (UK) Limited.
Large Print edition 2012
Harlequin (UK) Limited, Eton House,
18-24 Paradise Road, Richmond, Surrey TW9 1SR

© Dianne Despain 2012

ISBN: 978 0 263 22485 6

Harlequin (UK) policy is to use papers that are natural, renewable and recyclable products and made from wood grown in sustainable forests. The logging and manufacturing process conform to the legal environmental regulations of the country of origin.

Printed and bound in Great Britain
by CPI Antony Rowe, Chippenham, Wiltshire

She glanced over at him, simply studied him for a fraction of a second and then, without a word, turned her attention back to the dirt road and the never-ending expanse of nothingness stretching out in front of them.

But in that fraction of a second he felt... There weren't any words to describe it, really. Except she'd looked not into his soul but through it, and it shook him. Shook him bad.

"For us," he conceded. "And for our son. I really want to make this work, Belle. We may not be married, but Michael needs consistency from us...together."

Dear Reader

When I approached my editor with an idea to write a story featuring a child with Asperger's Syndrome, Mills & Boon® stood behind me solidly—for which I'm grateful. Asperger's has become popularised in fiction lately. I knew some of the overall facts, but after I began the deep research I needed for this book what I discovered was that every piece of information written about Asperger's Syndrome was basically the same: a laundry list of traits.

Then I met Chris who, with his Asperger's Syndrome, pretty much defies everything on the experts' list. And Chris is where the idea for my story went—from that laundry list of traits to the real face of Asperger's Syndrome. Musician, composer, poet, computer tech, athlete, scholar…you won't find those on the lists, but that's who Chris is—as well as a guy who absolutely makes direct eye contact and has a wicked, funny sense of humour. While he's not the character Michael I created, Chris inspired me to find that little boy—and, amazingly, what I discovered is that my Michael is pretty much like every other seven-year-old boy.

I think we tend to believe the lists, no matter what the situation or diagnosed condition. But Michael is an athlete, a computer genius, he loves bugs, plays games, has a passion for pizza, and the desperate wish of his heart is that his mom and dad would get back together. He's a kid with a plan.

Michael is also a kid with parents who love him more than anything in the world, and who are both trying hard to give him the support he'll need in the struggles he'll face in life. It's through Michael's eyes that they finally see themselves.

As always, wishing you health and happiness.

Dianne Drake

www.DianneDrake.com

Now that her children have left home, **Dianne Drake** is finally finding the time to do some of the things she adores—gardening, cooking, reading, shopping for antiques. Her absolute passion in life, however, is adopting abandoned and abused animals. Right now Dianne and her husband, Joel, have a little menagerie of three dogs and two cats, but that's always subject to change. A former symphony orchestra member, Dianne now attends the symphony as a spectator several times a month and, when time permits, takes in an occasional football, basketball or hockey game.

Recent titles by Dianne Drake:

THE RUNAWAY NURSE
FIREFIGHTER WITH A FROZEN HEART
THE DOCTOR'S REASON TO STAY**
FROM BROODING BOSS TO ADORING DAD
THE BABY WHO STOLE THE DOCTOR'S HEART*
CHRISTMAS MIRACLE: A FAMILY*
HIS MOTHERLESS LITTLE TWINS*

**New York Hospital Heartthrobs*
Mountain Village Hospital

These books are also available in eBook format from www.millsandboon.co.uk

To Chris, one of the people I love most.
You make the world a better place.

CHAPTER ONE

"ANYONE else?" Dr. Belle Carter called out to the ten or so ranch hands standing around, gawking at her. She was used to men gawking, but not like this bunch was doing. They were queasy, some of them wobbling on their feet, grabbing on to furniture, hugging walls. If there was a particular shade of color common to the sickly lot presently resisting her, she'd call it gray-green. But food poisoning did that, even in slight cases. Today, the old *E. coli* bug had struck down half the crew who worked on the Chachalaca Creek Ranch outside Big Badger, Texas. She'd suspected bad bean sprouts on the salad were the culprit when she'd sent the first samples to the lab for tests, though she was actually quite encouraged over a bunch of cowboys eating salads and not big, thick steaks or pork chops. Until all those cowboys let her take a look, she wasn't going to be sure about anything, though. "If you've still got any of the symptoms I've just described, or talked about the other times I was out here, you'd better tell me now. If you don't, it's going to knock you down, maybe for up to ten days. That's a promise." She held up a large bottle of pills, rattled it for effect. "Anti-nausea pills, if you're interested." Which nobody was. This was her third trip out here for this, and her last, if they continued to shun her the way they were doing.

"It's hard getting used to a new doc in town," Maudie Tucker, her nurse, said under her breath as she pulled Belle back from the men. "These boys are used to the way Doc Nelson used to do it, and having a lady doc makes them jumpy. They don't trust you yet."

They didn't trust her? That was clear. But they were sick, and in most cases sickness would override distrust. Not here apparently, and she was about to be bested by a bacterial gastric upset. "But Doc Nelson eloped with his thirty-five-years-his-junior receptionist, and I'm the only doctor within a hundred miles, so it's get used to the lady doctor or ride out the illness without my help," she whispered back, sympathetic to the men's plight and at the same time annoyed, watching them lope and drag themselves in single file into the next room over—the game room. Just to get away from her. As if she couldn't follow them and perform their exams on the pool table if she had to.

"It'll take them some time to adjust," Maudie replied. "Folks around here are cautious, but they'll get used to you—eventually."

"Eventually's not good enough. They're sick right now." Belle loved Maudie to pieces. She'd come with the medical practice, boasted forty-two years of hard-boiled nursing, and if she could she'd mother every one of Big Badger's citizens. Today, though, mothering wouldn't work. But a firm hand would, and she doubted Maudie had it in her to be firm with any of the ranch hands. "Which means they take the pills or..." She shrugged. "Some of them will probably get sicker, incur more time off work, and have to face the consequences when I explain to the ranch owner that they refused treatment—treatment he hired me to give." It also meant she was going to be the one to take a hard line here, if she intended on getting somewhere with the men. So she was going to chase them down, examine them, and treat them, whether or not they liked it. Good thing she was used to taking a hard line. Dr. Belle Carter, family practice specialist, had developed pretty thick skin over the course. Had had to, with what she'd gone through to get to this point in her life—tackling med school years later than many of her classmates, being a single mother, marriage to a man who'd spent most of their wedded years somewhere else. Married, past tense, naturally.

So today, with ten moderately sick people trying desperately to run away from her in their sluggardly sick gait, six appointments back at the office this afternoon, and flu vaccinations to give out later at the Salt Creek Ranch, she was extra-busy, and time was something she didn't have much of because at the end of it all she'd promised most of her evening to her son, Michael, and that was a promise she didn't want to break. He was the reason she was doing this, and doing it the hard way.

"My purpose here, my only purpose, is to have a look at each and every one of them, check their vital signs to make sure nothing else is going on and assess for dehydration or worsening symptoms, then treat what I find. It's a simple thing. Or it should be, if they'd let me do my job."

"Need some help?" a familiar voice asked from the doorway. "I don't have my medical bag with me this trip, but I can certainly help you with some of the process."

Anger was her first reaction to that voice. Then her heart skipped a beat. Then her lungs clutched, but only for a fraction of a second as when she caught her breath again she was right back at anger.

"What are you doing here, Cade?" she hissed, trying hard not to let the ranch hands overhear, even though every last one of them had now exited the room. "It's not your weekend. In fact, it's not even a weekend. So why are you here, bothering me, while I'm trying to do my job?"

"I'm here because I missed my favorite person in the world."

She swallowed hard, fighting to regain control as all the ranch hands in the other room, no matter how sick, were watching her, gauging her reaction, probably trying to find some argument to use against her when they were called out for refusing treatment. She sucked in a deep breath, squared her shoulders, steadied herself, and said, with all the calmness she could muster, "He's in school." Three words, so much effort. But Cade took effort.

Oh, they had an amicable situation where Michael was concerned. No one looking on could say otherwise. Twice a month Cade flew from Chicago to Texas to visit his son, and he never missed a date, never made excuses. He was diligent in that, something she actually admired in the man. In fact, she'd seen Cade more often in the two months she and Michael had lived in Texas than she had the last two months they'd lived a block down the street from him. He'd never missed his visitation then either. But in that situation it had been easier to avoid Cade, which she did as often as she could.

Now, though, with Cade showing up on her doorstep so often, coming from so far away, avoiding him wasn't all that easy. "And I don't need help taking care of my patients." Finally, now that the first flush of anger was under control, and nothing was skipping, clutching, or doing anything abnormal to her physiology, she turned to face him. "How did you know where to find me anyway?"

He looked straight at Maudie, who was blushing all kinds of red, and smiled. "I have a few friends here in Big Badger, Texas."

Dr. Cade Carter could sweet-talk the needles right off a prickly old cactus. He was a charmer, all right. Nothing about him had changed in that respect, and Maudie Tucker was the living proof. "Well, in case your friend didn't tell you, I've got a busy day ahead of me and I don't have time to waste standing here talking to you. But since you're here, for who knows what reason, you can see Michael after school. I'll call Virginia and let her know you'll be picking him up." Virginia Ellison, retired librarian, was Michael's caregiver, and the only person in Big Badger she really trusted with her son.

"Except it's not just Michael I came to see. Normally, when I'm here on my visitation weekends, there's not enough time or you're too busy. But we need to talk, Belle. There are some things I want to say, want to tell you, that don't fit into the regular schedule, and I was hoping..." He shrugged. "It's important. That's all I'm saying."

Now her heart skipped a beat again, and not in a good way. She'd had years of disappointments, one after another, from this man, and she was conditioned for it. But not here, not now, and that's all she could think this would be. Cade changing something, Cade doing something that would affect her life. The divorce, five years ago, had ended all the letdowns and she didn't want to go back to that. Not even for a minute. Yet it felt like that's exactly where Cade was trying to drag her now. Except nearly ten years of having Cade Carter in her life had taught her how to dig her heels in. But those same years of Cade Carter had also taught her just how vulnerable she could be to him, if she let herself.

"I'm working, Cade. Whatever you want, we'll do it later when I'm ready. And in the meantime, leave me alone."

"Fine, later. When you're ready. But in the meantime, it looks to me like you could use another doctor here."

She glanced into the next room at her patients, who all seemed to have lost interest in the interchange between Cade and herself, then took two steps closer to Cade. Gritted her teeth. Whispered,

"Don't do this to me in front of my patients, Cade Carter. Do not undermine my abilities by implying that I can't do my job without your help. So get out of here and leave me alone."

"I was just offering," he said, not budging.

Just offering. But what was he really offering here? That's what had her stumped. They'd been divorced five years now, and she'd been relieved to see it end when it had. Sure, it had been sad, in so many ways. Especially because of Michael. But she couldn't have survived with Cade. She'd needed more, he'd needed less. "Fine. We'll talk later. Whatever kind of bad news you're going to spring on me can wait until I've finished my day."

"I never meant to do that to you, you know?"

"Do what?"

"Make you think the worst of me. Or anticipate that anything I have to say to you is bad news."

"I don't think the worst of you, Cade. But we were married, remember? I got used to having the worst of you."

"And sometimes the best." He cocked a half-smile, stepped back, tipped his cowboy hat at her. "Later," he said, then turned and walked off.

"Surprised you'd let him get away," Maudie

commented, watching him almost as hard as Belle was.

"You can't keep someone who doesn't want to be kept, Maudie," she said, turning back to the group of men she'd come to treat. Now, though, her mind was on Cade. Good dad. First-rate surgeon. And the last person she'd expected to see when he wasn't scheduled for a weekend with Michael. But Cade was up to something. She knew it, felt it, didn't know what it was, and that's what she had to get her mind off right now.

"OK, everybody," Belle said, fighting to refocus on her patients. "Here's the deal. I've got a kid to support. He's seven. I don't have a lot of time to spend with him, and the longer it takes here, the less time Michael and I are going to have. So you can fight me on this, refuse to let me check you, but it's affecting my son. Any of you have children you'd like to spend more time with, or mothers who'd love spending more time with you? Because if you do, then you'll understand what I'm talking about, and get in line so I can get this done as quickly as possible."

"Ah, the sentimental touch. Well done," Maudie

joked as, one by one, the men started to trickle forward.

Belle laughed. "Whatever it takes." She wondered what it would take with Cade. Surely he wanted something she didn't want to give. Quite the opposite from their marriage, where she'd wanted something he hadn't wanted to give. Definitely, whatever it takes, she thought to herself.

Two hours later Belle was pleased with the results of her morning. All but three ranch hands had eventually fallen in line. This evening, once the nausea pills took effect, all but three ranch hands would feel better. Had she gained any respect from these men? Nah. She wasn't that deluded. They'd sympathized either as a father or a son. It was good enough for now. Battle number one went to the lady doctor. Battle number two coming up, though, with Cade? No, she didn't know for sure there was going to be a battle between them, but she was clearly feeling something in the pit of her stomach, and it made her nervous, as the only thing she could think that Cade would want was Michael.

* * *

"Didn't mean to put you in a spot," Cade said, as Belle stepped out of her car.

"That's an apology?"

"If you need one then, yes, it's an apology."

He was leaning up against the entrance to her office, standing in the shade, cowboy hat tipped low over his face. Admittedly, he still took away her breath. A sexier, better-looking man God had never put on the face of this earth, and she responded to that in huge ways. Dark brown hair just slightly wavy, slate-gray eyes. Tall, muscled physique of a god. She'd responded to it too quickly all those years ago, jumping into his bed the first opportunity she'd had, then into marriage at approximately the same irresponsible speed. "What's with the hat?" She'd never seen him in a cowboy hat before today, but it did him justice. If anything, it made him look sexier.

"When in Texas." He tilted the brim back. Stared her in the eye. "Since you're raising my son to be a cowboy now."

"Apology accepted, but don't ever do that to me again, Cade," she warned, brushing by him to unlock the door. "I'm having a hard enough time as it is, establishing myself here in the wake of the legendary Dr. Nelson, and I don't need you step-ping in to help me, or whatever it was you were trying to do out there on the Chachalaca. And why are you here anyway? You just left three days ago, and you're not due back for—"

"Nine more days, which is why I'm here now. Nine days is a long time. Too long."

That feeling in the pit of her stomach turned into a hard knot as the hint of a custody battle took on stronger overtones. Cade had never fought her on her being custodial parent, so why now? "Meaning?" she asked, struggling not to sound as apprehensive as she felt.

"Meaning I don't get enough time with Michael. He's growing up, and every other weekend isn't working for me. You've been gone two months, Belle, and the arrangement is driving me crazy. So I decided to take a few weeks off my practice and hang around Big Badger, see what's rocking his world these days. Discover things I can't dis-cover in my allotted few hours of visitation."

"Why now, Cade? It's been this way for five years, so why now?"

"Because I'm getting older."

She shook her head. "That's not it."

"Maybe there's not one certain 'it', Belle. Maybe I just want to be included more."

Like he'd wanted to be included in their marriage, but hardly ever showed up for it? Like he'd wanted to be included in so many of the other milestones they should have been celebrating as a family, only Cade had always, conveniently, been missing from them? Cade had been the consummate husband in absentia, so why this? And why now? "You're not sick, are you? A terminal illness, or something life-threatening?"

He chuckled. "You always were straight to the point but, no, I'm not sick. Does that disappoint you?"

"Believe it or not, Cade, I don't hate you. Never have, and unless you give me cause, like taking Michael away from me, I never will."

"Is that what you think? That I'm here to take Michael away from you?"

"Seems logical, doesn't it? Things are going along fine then, out of the blue, you're here, telling me you want to make changes. So is that what it's about, Cade? Do you want to take Michael away from me?"

"What I want, what I've always wanted, is

what's best for him. That's you, Belle. I wouldn't take him away from you, and I'm sorry you'd think I would." He shook his head. "That's the second time I've apologized for causing you to think the worst of me. It's not how I want it to be between us, you know."

She was relieved. Still curious, since Cade was acting so out of character. But very relieved. "I know, and neither do I. And for what it's worth, I really didn't think you would take him from me. We've had our bad moments, Cade, but I didn't think you'd do that. It's just that you showing up here the way you have makes me uncomfortable. I don't know what to expect."

"And in your life you always like to know what to expect." It was said with no malicious intent whatsoever.

"It's who I am." And part of the reason their marriage had failed. Cade never had understood that in her. "So anyway, I know you miss Michael, but what's the real reason you're here?"

"That is the real reason. Can't it be just that simple?"

She shook her head, then gestured for him to follow her through to the exam rooms and into her private office, trying not to think about how Cade was still on the verge of something that, try as she did to fight it, made her feel anxious. "So, on a whim, you can just walk away from your surgical practice?" she asked, shutting the door behind her and grappling for something, anything, to steady her nerves. A deep breath, a sturdy wall to lean on. Amicable divorce, yes, amicable parenting arrangements, yes. But there was nothing amicable about the way she was feeling as this was all about Cade wanting to change her life again, no matter how simple he claimed this matter of his was going to be. "You can just decide you don't want to work then fly to Texas for a day or two?"

"Actually, like I said a minute ago, I'm here for a few weeks. That's one of the advantages of being co-owner of a growing surgical practice. You get to make the rules. And since there are always a dozen or so other surgeons to cover for me, I decided I needed—well, you can believe what you want, but I came to spend some time with Michael."

"Really? A few weeks?" This was making less and less sense by the minute. "You're going to stay in Big Badger for a few weeks?" Normally, Cade was one step shy of arrogance, but she didn't see that in his eyes. They were the eyes that kept him hidden, blocked the light from his soul. Not now, though. Cade was not only serious about staying here, he was emotionally invested in it.

"Seriously, Belle, is wanting more time with my son such a bad thing?"

Under most circumstances, no. And she didn't know what to think about this now. Except she'd seen that flicker of emotion in his eyes just then. Brief, but definitely there. The same flicker of emotion she'd seen the day Michael had been born, same flicker she'd seen the day she'd told Cade that Michael had been diagnosed with Asperger's syndrome. Cade Carter kept most of himself hidden, but not always. And those un-hidden moments were always genuine. She knew that with all her heart. "OK, I understand that you're not going to tell me everything, and I don't have time to stand here and try arguing it out of you. I do think you want to see Michael, and for now I'm going to leave it at that. But later, Cade. We're going to deal with this—this whatever it is—whether or not you like it."

"I swear, it's all about Michael," he said, putting on the old Cade grin. The charmer grin that had got her into trouble in the first place. "And since we have an open agreement about him—"

"Before you make any more plans, I've made arrangements for him in Austin for the next three weeks. It's a good program. It's gained lots of awards for its advances in autism, and is headed by a doctor who's internationally known for her work."

"Which he doesn't need to go to now that I'm here to spend that time with him."

"But it's arranged."

"And I don't remember you asking me about it."

"OK, maybe I should have asked, like you should have asked before just showing up here unannounced. But a month ago, when I told you I wanted to talk to you about a program I'd found for him, you said you'd get back to me. Said that to me each of the three other times I tried talking to you about it. Remember that?"

He drew in a stiff breath. "I was busy."

"I was, too." Now the charm had dissolved, and they were back to the same old problems. "But I made the time to investigate the program, and made the time to try and get you to listen to me about it. But you weren't listening at all, were you? That's why you're here now. Because you didn't hear a word I said, sort of like the way it was when we were married." There was no disputing they both wanted what was best for their son, but that's where the co-operation stopped. Cade had his ideas, which were, basically, more love and more involvement could cure anything. She had hers, which were to find her son the best available programs for children with Asperger's syndrome. That didn't preclude more love and more involvement. It merely gave Michael one more shot at having a better life. "So I hope you bought a round-trip ticket, because if you hurry, you can be back in Chicago by tonight."

"Unenroll him. I want to spend the next few weeks with him."

"No, I'm not going to unenroll him. You've got Michael six straight weeks at the end of summer, and that's all you're getting, so deal with it. Go home, leave me alone." Arrangements had already been made for Cade to take Michael back to Chicago with him, which she didn't like but which she hoped would be good for her son. Unlike Cade, she had no intention of stepping in and trying to upset things. Michael's life was a precarious balance, and he didn't need the disruption.

"And what I've been telling you is that six weeks aren't enough, Belle. I miss him. It's driving me crazy, knowing I can't see Michael whenever I want to. Getting him for three-day weekends every other week and every other holiday isn't cutting it. And half that time is spent in transit, flying down here to be with him and flying back to be home on time for my Monday morning surgeries. And, really, how much time do I get to spend with him when I'm here? Have you ever thought about it, Belle? Three, maybe four hours total, adjusting to his schedule and routines, as well as his attention span? Which is why I want to spend the whole summer with him, and not just part of it." He drew in a ragged breath. "I need to connect better with my boy and teach him to connect better with me."

She did have to admit Cade was the one who got cheated, especially as she was the one who'd moved from Chicago to Big Badger, breaking up a perfectly good custody arrangement, one much more conducive to Cade's situation. But he was the Texas boy after all. The cowboy who'd spent every day of their marriage talking about how great Texas was, how he wanted to move back someday, how it was the best place in the country to raise kids.

Well, she'd listened. More than that, she'd believed. So now here she was, raising their kid in Texas. And here Cade wasn't, except for his every-other-week visitations. "Look, it's only a three-week program, Cade. You can have the three weeks after it's over, here in Big Badger, though. And that would still give you more time than we'd originally planned."

"But I want more than that," he repeated, stubbornly.

"Without notice."

"Because there was no notice to give. I decided to do this…" he glanced at his watch "…ten hours ago. Ten hours, Belle. I changed my life in the last ten hours because I miss my son. And I think spending the next few weeks with me will be better for Michael than sending him off into some program."

Even if it was an excellent program, letting Michael spend time with his dad was the better situation. No argument there. And having Cade here would be wonderful for Michael. Still, one of the reasons she'd chosen to move to godforsaken Big Badger was to be close to Dr. Amanda Robinson. Sure, the town had made her an offer she couldn't refuse, but it was one of three amazing offers that had come at her. The decision had come down to Amanda's excellent reputation in autism. She worked miracles with kids no one expected miracles from, and to be so close to all that was why she was working in a town that didn't want a lady doctor, and being on call to a bunch of hostile ranch hands. Yet nothing Amanda could or would do would substitute for the fact that Michael needed his father, and that's what ultimately changed Belle's mind. Not Cade's need, but Michael's. "OK. If you're really going to stay here, I'll pull him out of the program. But there's a three-day trip he's been begging to go on, and I'm not cancelling that, no matter what you say. Dr. Robinson is doing good things for Michael and I don't want to cause problems with that."

"You think that highly of the good doctor's program?"

"I do. Michael needs that kind of professional

guidance and I need that kind of personal support. With Amanda, we get both."

"Good. Then I can live with that."

But could she? Big Badger was a small town, there wasn't much to do here. And she could envision herself bumping into Cade every time she turned around for the next six weeks. Bumps she didn't want to be making. "It's not about what you can live with," she snapped. "It's about what's best for Michael. Dr. Robinson's part of it, but you're a bigger part." He'd spent their married life staying away, and she'd got used to it. Got used to the distances in their divorce, too, and she wasn't sure what having him around all the time was going to do to her. But for Michael… "And you're not staying with me."

"Didn't intend to. I took a room at the boarding house. Paid for the full six weeks."

He smiled, arched ridiculously sexy eyebrows— the whole Cade effect that had always been her downfall.

"Cade Carter, staying in a boarding house and not some luxurious hotel suite?" Belle raised her eyebrows over that one, because it told her, whatever his reason, he was dead serious about spending more time with Michael.

"Find me a luxurious hotel in Big Badger, and I'll check in."

"And you're still not going to tell me what this is really about?" There wasn't a casual explanation. Knowing Cade, there couldn't be. But Cade honestly loved Michael, even though Michael didn't give much back to his dad. So maybe it was about Cade feeling excluded or unloved? Certainly, that's how she would feel if Michael was as unresponsive to her as he was to Cade. So she hoped that was the simple explanation after all.

But there'd been a time when she'd hoped so many things about Cade, and look where that had got her.

"I can tell you a thousand times a day for the next six weeks. My being here is about spending more time with Michael. That's all, Belladonna."

Nope. She knew Cade, and she didn't buy it. But, as they said, forewarned was forearmed. Only she didn't know against what. "Fine. You've got your extra six weeks. And don't call me Belladonna." Meaning beautiful woman, or deadly nightshade, take your pick. It used to be his pet name for her, used when he'd wanted to get his way. Which he'd just done, hadn't he?

The charmer grin grew larger as Cade tilted his hat back down over his eyes. "Anybody ever tell you you're a real pushover, Belle Carter?"

Nobody had to tell her. When it came to Cade Carter, she always had been. Looked like that hadn't changed too much either. "All the time," she said, opening her office door and gesturing him to leave. "All the time."

Belle watched him amble down the hall and out the back office door, admiring that same swagger she'd always admired. "So, what are you up to, Cade?" she asked, under her breath, as she shrugged into her white lab coat and headed off to see her first patient of the afternoon. "What are you really up to?" And how was she going to stay resistant to it? That was the big question.

"How would you like to spend more time with your dad this summer, Michael?" Kicking her shoes to the other side of the room, Belle dropped back onto the sofa and lay there, flat on her back, staring up at the ceiling. "Michael," she said again, without glancing over. She knew what he was doing. Playing video games. The love of his life. Lately, though, he hadn't been playing them so much as creating one of his own, doing preliminary sketches, working out the story details. "Did you hear me? I asked if you'd like to spend more time with your dad this summer."

"Yeah," Michael said, his rapt attention still fixed on his game.

"Well, he's here. In Big Badger." Not that telling him would make a difference, but he did process the information. Just not always on the spot. "And he wants to spend the summer with you. So you'll have to start thinking about all the things you'd like to do with him, maybe make a list. OK?"

"Yeah," he said.

Belle was sure he was simply telling her what she wanted to hear, and paying absolutely no attention to her at the same time. Complex mind. So complex that it scared her sometimes. Most of the time, though, she didn't think about it. Because to Michael she was only Mom, doing the mom things she was supposed to do. Like making dinner. Her next chore. "What do you want to eat?" she asked him, then added, before he answered,

"Not pizza. We've had that two night in a row now. So, what else?"

"Pizza," he said anyway.

She wasn't sure if that was because pizza was truly his favorite food or if it was simply what came to mind first, turning it into the easiest way to respond to her yet still stay focused on what he was doing. "No pizza," she said emphatically.

"OK." He turned to her, grinning. "Fried chicken, mashed potatoes without lumps with white gravy without lumps, corn on the cob and homemade biscuits. With honey."

Belle moaned, then laughed. He did this on purpose—his sense of humor. Michael knew she couldn't cook, at least not that kind of meal. And he teased her about it. "You mean hamburgers, don't you? On the grill?"

"Can I cook them?" he asked.

"Do pigs fly?" she asked, teasing him.

"Only in another universe, Mom," he said, then turned back to his game.

"When you say something cute like that, you know what I'm going to have to do, don't you?"

"No!" he squealed, curling himself into a ball. "Not that!"

Belle rolled off the couch then crawled on hands and knees across the floor to Michael, who was rolling away from her. "Yes, that! The cuddle game. You know how much I love the cuddle game." Her cuddle game was a form of hug therapy used on children who had an aversion to being touched, like Michael had had when he'd been younger. It was one of several sensory issues she'd been dealing with, along with loud noises and some bright colors. It had taken Belle years to get him to the point where accepting physical affection was a pleasant experience for him. Sometimes, even now, she wasn't sure if it was or if he was merely putting on an act to placate her. Either way, it didn't matter. A few minutes to cuddle her son meant everything. Everything.

"Can he come to dinner?" Michael asked, before Belle had even gotten all the way over to him.

Of all things, that was the one question that stopped her dead, threw that bucket of water on the cuddle game. Could Cade come to dinner? Her first response was, *When pigs fly!* She didn't want to spend the evening with Cade. Didn't particularly even want to be in the same room with him. But this was Michael asking. Michael, who never asked for anything except more RAM for his computer. "Well, I have a better idea than that. Why don't I call your dad and see if he'll come take you out for pizza?" Which was exactly what she did, when Michael's attention, once again, returned to his game.

"He wants pizza, he wants you," she said to Cade, when he answered his phone. "And what's with the pickup truck I saw you in earlier?" A sleek, low-riding sports car was more his style.

"Had to rent something."

"Well, Michael's never been in a pickup truck so I don't know if that's going to work. You can leave it here and borrow my car."

"Or I can leave your car right where it is and take him in the truck. Or would the two of you rather meet me somewhere?"

"I prefer the sound of a boys' night out, while I take a long, hot bath and finish that mystery novel I've been trying to finish for the last month." A night that might have, under different circumstances, been perfect. Tonight, though, the image of a cozy little family of three eating pizza together popped into her thoughts, making her feel, well, not sad for the present so much as sad for the things they'd had in the past. It seemed like such a long time ago. So far away it was difficult trying to remember when they'd been happy. They had been, though. In the early years, when Michael had still been a baby and she had been plunking along through medical school a little at a time, trying to balance motherhood and career. Good times for a while. So many hopes and dreams. Bright futures in the planning. But with a supportive husband for only such a short while before he'd started retreating. "Oh, and I've told Michael you're going to be here for a while, and to get a list ready of things he wants to do with you. And before you tell me there's nothing he wants to do with you, you're wrong. There are a lot of things. You have to be patient, getting him to tell you."

"But he will," Cade replied. "Isn't that what you always tell me? Be patient, and he'll do it. Except he never does, Belle. Never does."

He did, though. Cade simply wasn't very good at picking up on the subtle signs. The irony was that that was a typical Asperger's symptom. Only thing was, while Michael had Asperger's, Cade did not. And it was Cade's lack in that area that was, in part, responsible for the death of their marriage. "Then work on it. And, please, not video games and computers. He gets enough of that in his day-to-day life, and he really needs something else."

"In Big Badger, Texas? What else is there, Belle? You pretty much came to the end of the earth with this job, and I can't see this place being exactly stimulating for a child."

"In Big Badger, Texas, you have to use your imagination. Get used to it, Cade. You're the one who chose to spend six weeks here." She thought she heard a groan on the other end of the phone. She smiled. "Pick him up in an hour. And make sure he wears his seat belt in that truck. He's in a new phase where the seat belt bothers him, and he'll take it off if he thinks you're not watching. So watch him!"

"Anybody ever tell you to lighten up?"

"Anybody ever tell you that we're divorced and I'm none of your business any more?" Still smiling, she clicked off. But rather than being angry, she was wondering if having Cade around for a while might be good. Definitely for Michael, but maybe a little bit for her, too? Funny thing was, since the moment she'd heard his voice out there on the Chachalaca, she'd had this peculiar feeling in the pit of her stomach. Suddenly, it was gone.

CHAPTER TWO

OK, so maybe it wasn't the smartest thing he'd ever done, taking a leave of absence and coming to Texas. Not the most thought-out either, since he'd done it on the spur of the moment. But, damn it, he missed Michael. For all the rough patches in their relationship, and there were plenty of them, his kid was his life, and he hated it that he couldn't see him any time, like he'd done before Belle had moved to Big Badger.

It was about his brother Robbie, too. It was his birthday today. That was another regret, realizing how much he'd missed. And guilt. Feeling it more acutely as the years rolled on. Recognizing he was well on that track with Michael, too.

So he'd endure Big Badger for a few weeks, see what he really wanted to do after that, and the trade-off for the things he hadn't figured out yet was extra time to spend with Michael while he was traveling through yet another undecided phase of his life. Maybe, just maybe, he'd find a way to relate to his son better or, at the very least, get Michael to respond to him.

Spending time with Belle was also something he'd given a lot of thought to. He'd caused the divorce. There was no other way to look at it. She'd needed a husband, and he'd needed—well, he still didn't know the answer to that, did he? But whatever it was, he owed Belle in a big way for the letdown of a husband he'd been, and while he couldn't make that up to her, he could make some amends by being a better father.

How? He wasn't sure. There weren't many options open to him. But somewhere inside those next six weeks, maybe he'd prove himself to Michael, and also to Belle, by showing how he was more than the father who simply appeared at the door to pick up his kid every couple of weeks. What would he get from Belle in return? He didn't have a clue, but he was willing to take anything. Michael needed that. So did he. Because those were some feelings he had to resolve as well while he was here.

Tall order to fulfill—better dad, better ex-husband. To move forward, though, that was his agenda, otherwise he'd have to step away from them altogether, for Michael's sake, he told himself. Whatever he did, it had to be for Michael's sake. And for Belle's. Because, God knew, he didn't deserve anything for his own sake.

"So, what kind of pizza do you want?" he asked Michael, as they headed to the truck.

"Mom coming?" Michael asked, trailing along behind Cade by a good ten large steps.

"Mom's tired tonight. So it's only going to be the two of us." Not the best choice of words apparently, because once Michael heard them he stopped, then turned around and headed back to Belle's front door. A purposeful march, and a very obvious one. Michael wanted his mother, not his dad. Understanding that, Cade felt his heart fall.

"I'll get her," Michael said.

"But she doesn't want to come." Neither did Michael.

"That's OK. She likes pizza, too. Just not every night."

With that, Michael disappeared back into the house, leaving Cade standing alone on the sidewalk. Feeling rotten. Inadequate. Feeling like an idiot for not knowing what to do now. Should he go after Michael, insist that pizza was only for the two of them? Ask Belle to come along to make the situation better? These were the things that eluded him, the things he should know how to manage. But didn't.

"See, this is the way it always is," he said, clearly frustrated when Belle appeared at the door with Michael in hand.

"I explained it, and now Michael understands that I'm not part of the pizza party tonight. He was just afraid that I might not fix myself anything for dinner."

It was more than that. It was Michael showing concern for his mother in a way Cade had never seen. Or had never felt from Michael himself. It was a proud moment, seeing that in his son, yet a profoundly sad one as well. To Belle's credit, though, for being such a good mother to Michael. "And will you?"

Belle shook her head. "Too tired. I'll grab an apple, maybe some yogurt, and I'll be good." She scooted Michael out the door, then took a step back. "So you two have fun tonight. And I'll see you in a couple of hours."

"Sure you don't want to come with us?" Cade called.

"Sure," she said, shutting the door.

This time she locked it. Cade heard the bolt latch. "OK, then. It really is just the two of us." And a whole summer ahead, with more of this. On top of which, he was going to be with Belle. Now, that was going to be the bigger challenge. Belle Elise Foster Carter—the best of his life while he was the worst of hers. Yes, she was definitely going to be the biggest challenge he was going to face in Big Badger, Texas.

"So tell me about school," Cade said, handing a slice of pizza, pepperoni only, over to his son.

"It's OK," Michael replied, his attention fixed squarely on a floor-sized video game in the corner of the restaurant—a road-race game meant for kids twice his age.

"Is math still your favorite subject?"

"Um, yes."

"Still like your science classes?"

"Uh-huh."

It was clear Michael was more interested in the game than his dad, and Cade understood that.

Still, it was frustrating not being able to hold his son's attention for more than a fraction of a second, basically losing out to a game, and he was fighting to keep in his nettled sigh. Belle had the relationship with Michael he wanted. He was glad for her. But it bothered the hell out of him that, no matter how hard he tried with Michael, he was barely on his son's radar. "Want to go play?" he finally asked, giving in to the obvious.

Michael nodded his head and, for a second, glanced at Cade. His expression was...happy? Did he see happiness in his son's eyes, or was that merely wishful thinking? As quickly as Michael looked over, though, he looked away. Right back at the video game.

"After you finish your pizza," Cade said. "Deal?"

Michael nodded. "Deal." Then he crammed the rest of his pizza into his mouth, so much so his cheeks bulged as he tried to chew it and swallow. Finally, his mouth cleared, he held out his hand to Cade. "Money, please."

"How much?" Cade asked, not expecting an answer.

"It's a dollar a game. Can I play ten games? Because that would be ten dollars."

Explained very seriously. But it was the most Michael had said all evening and for that Cade rewarded him with ten dollars. For a moment it crossed his mind to go play the game with Michael, but he knew that would cause his son more frustration than he could deal with, so he twisted his chair to watch, then leaned back to make himself more comfortable. "I'll save you some pizza for later," he said, before Michael scampered off.

"Thanks, Dad," he said, clutching the handful of dollar bills like they were a lifesaving elixir.

Cade blinked his surprise. "You're welcome. Oh, and, Michael…" he called, as Michael was already halfway across the room. "Have fun."

"It was nice, hearing him call you Dad," Belle said, settling into the chair next to Cade.

"Thought you were staying home."

"Turns out I can't."

"Because you don't think I can take good care of our son?" he asked. "Because you want to see, in action, how you're the good mom and I'm the bad dad?"

Immediately, Belle bristled. "Don't go there, Cade. I didn't come down here to fight with you. I've got to go out to the Chachalaca again, to see a couple of the holdouts. The ranch owner threatened them with their jobs and now they're willing to let the lady doc treat them. So don't hassle me. This is my fourth time out there, and I'm not happy about it."

"I could go," he offered. "Seriously. You could take the rest of the night off, maybe stay here and finish the pizza, and I could go out to the Chachalaca."

"Trying to make amends is nice, Cade, and I appreciate it. But duty calls, and this duty is mine. What I was wondering, though, is when you take Michael home later on, would you mind staying there with him until I get back? If you can't, that's fine. I can call Virginia Ellison, and she'll be glad—"

"Not a problem," he said, sliding the pizza box over toward Belle. "If it gets too late, I'll sleep on the couch. Care for a slice to take with you?"

She laughed. "Between you and me, I really hate pizza. But Michael loves it, and sometimes it's the only thing I can get him to eat."

He pulled the pizza back and took a large slice for himself, one dripping with pizza sauce and cheese. "You're the one who worked with him on calling me Dad, aren't you?"

"I know it's difficult for you, not getting to see him more, then when you do it takes him so long to warm up to you. So I thought—"

He held up his hand to stop her, then swallowed the bite in his mouth. "I appreciate it, even if it doesn't come naturally to him. And what I just said about you coming here to watch me be the bad dad…" He sighed. "You are the good mom, you know. Sometimes when I see that, and see how Michael responds to you—it bothers me, Belle. And it bothers me that you had to teach my son to call me Dad. I loved hearing him say it, but I would have loved it even more if it had been spontaneous."

"I think it was. Normally, I prompt him before your weekends. Just mention it once or twice. But this isn't one of your weekends, and what's happening now is totally off Michael's routine. So I didn't prompt him."

Cade smiled, but didn't respond, because he knew Belle was wrong. It was her work that had brought about Michael's efforts. More than that, it made him feel terrible that, even in divorce, Belle cared more about his feelings than he'd ever cared about hers while they'd been married.

"Anyway…" She scooted back her chair to leave, then turned and waved to Michael, who took a moment to glance up from his game in progress. "I've got to go. So I'm going to go tell Michael where I'll be while you polish off all that pizza, because he's too caught up in his game to want any more of it." She stepped away, stopped, then turned back to him. "You still got the six-pack?" Referring to his rock-hard abs.

The question totally surprised him. And intrigued him. "Why?"

"Just a warning about what can come from too many nights in the pizza parlor. And if Michael has his way with you, you'll be here every night." She smiled. "It would be a pity to mess up one of the good things about you, Cade."

"Sounds like you almost care."

"You had nice abs. That's all I'm saying." Then, finally, she walked away.

He watched, didn't budge an inch to stand and be polite, or even walk along with her over to

Michael. Belle, with her honey-blonde hair and sassy green eyes. And a sway to her hips that begged his stare. She was sexy as hell. Always had been, always would be. That's what caught him first glance, but what reeled him in was her intelligence, and her overall zest for life. Belle did life in a big way, bigger than anybody he'd ever met in his life. So straightforward about it, too, like she'd been just then. She still remembered liking his abs? He wasn't sure how to take it. Maybe as a compliment, maybe as a warning, like she'd said.

Or maybe—nah, he wasn't going there. He had friends who'd told him sex with the ex after the divorce was awesome. Maybe it was, he didn't know. But Belle wasn't the type. And, truly, he'd never even thought about it until just now. Well, maybe he had thought about it a time or two. But not seriously. And what she'd said about his abs— that was Belle being her straightforward self, giving him a warning and letting him know, in her own way, he was going to get a lot of time with Michael. Yes, that's what she'd meant. He was sure of it. Positive. Well, almost positive.

Still thinking about Belle as she lingered a moment to watch Michael's game, he knew now what he'd always known—nobody compared. Nobody even came close. In fact, the skinny list of women he'd considered dating from time to time were either so boring, bland, or so inane, trite, or shallow he never got around to the asking-out stage. Truth was, he hadn't dated because nobody seemed—well, like Belle. Not that he'd ever date her again, or do anything else with her, because he'd messed that up in the worst way a man could mess up the best thing in his life. But in a woman he needed personality and drive and, so far, he hadn't found that in any way that suited him other than in Belle, and that didn't count any more.

Which was fine, for now, as he wasn't in any hurry to settle down again. Of course, some people, Belle specifically, would argue he'd never settled down in the first place. "Look," he said, jumping into her path as she whooshed by him on her way out the door, "I don't want to fight. OK? It seems like we're always fighting, or just on the verge of it, and I don't want us doing that."

"Neither do I, but we're so good at it," she said, smiling. "I'd hate to give up on a good thing."

He chuckled, in spite of himself. "That's the thing I fell in love with, you know?"

"What?" she asked. "That I defend myself? That I stand up to you, face-to-face, and punch back?"

"Well, that could be part of the charm—for someone else. But what drew me to you was your fire. Just not so much of it. Anyway, that accusation a few minutes ago—it was a cheap shot. Totally uncalled-for, and I'm sorry. But sometimes—"

"Look, I do understand. It's not easy being Michael's dad, and it's probably not easy being my ex—although I'm not sure why it isn't, because I think I'm pretty easy to get along with." This time her smile was a tease. "Anyway, I've got to make my house call and these ranch hands aren't happy about it, so I just want to get out there and get it over with. Michael knows you're going to spend the evening with him, and that I might be late. He understands. So…" She shrugged, then hurried out the restaurant door, leaving Cade to watch her until she climbed into her car and drove away.

Yep, she certainly had fire. And if he was not mistaken, the flames had shot up a notch or two since they'd divorced. It was not unattractive in her, he decided as he ambled over to Michael and watched him trounce the evildoers in his game. Trounce, like a pro.

Damn, if his kid wasn't good at it! "So, Michael. Want to show me what you're doing?"

Michael didn't take his eyes off the screen, didn't even miss a shot. "Um, no."

The sting of that one word rocked him back a couple of steps. But that's as far as he went. Then he stood his ground, the way Belle would, and watched his son accomplish the highest score ever achieved on that particular game machine without breaking a sweat. How the hell was he ever going to make the score with Michael, with or without sweat?

That was the question he'd been asking himself for years. It was also the question for which he couldn't find an answer.

Then it hit him. Michael had called him Dad. Maybe prompted, maybe not. But—Dad. The most beautiful word he'd ever heard. So maybe there wasn't an answer to his question, except patience. And time.

The big problem, though, was distance, and there was no way to get around that.

He looked so innocent sleeping. So beautiful. She'd always thought that. And in their last year together, after so much struggling, she'd thought it was a pity he didn't sleep more often, because when he woke up, life changed. Fighting, bitterness—the emptiness of long, lonely hours by herself. Cade had caused her the kind of unhappiness she'd never thought would be part of her life. Yet she understood. Part of it came with his frustration over Michael. It hurt him, being ignored by a son he loved so deeply. But part of it was his absence, which was something she'd never understood and which, in retrospect, she wished she'd pursued with him until he'd explained it. His need, or lust, to leave had started mere weeks after they'd pronounced their vows, and had only got worse with time. She'd hoped it was a phase, some kind of life adjustment she just didn't understand. But it hadn't been, and when she'd asked him to explain, to help her understand, she'd been met with Cade's characteristic wall of resistance. So after a while, being rebuffed every time she asked, she quit asking, essentially giving up as it was clear that she was moving forward with her life and her husband was moving away.

Oh, sure. Cade had his causes—causes she admired. Sadly, at the time, his family hadn't seemed one of them. Maybe it was because she was strong and he'd believed she could hold things together in his absence. Maybe he found more satisfaction helping others than he did helping his family. All these years later she still didn't know why. But now she didn't dwell on it so much because her choice to move on without him, or get left behind, had been a good one.

Yet he still looked so innocent, sleeping. Like the man she'd fallen in love with all those years ago.

Belle smiled as she studied him. Michael looked so much like him. Same gray eyes, same dark brown hair, wavy with a little bit of curl. Same crooked smile. Except neither Michael nor Cade smiled much, which was a pity. Because it was a beautiful smile. One she'd wanted to capture in a family photo back when they'd been a family.

"It's late," Cade mumbled in his sleepy voice.

The sleepy voice—another thing she used to

love. It was a little thick, a little gruff. "Going on to midnight."

"Does it happen often?" he asked, propping himself up on one elbow.

"What? Me running around and leaving Michael here with a babysitter? Is that what you're asking me, Cade? Do I neglect my son on a regular nightly basis?" She hadn't meant to take offense, but sometimes Cade provoked that in her. Usually without much effort. Like now, when she was thinking about the things she'd planned with him—things she'd never have.

He stretched, sat up. Stretched again. "Actually, I wasn't thinking about Michael. It's you I was concerned about, being the only doctor for miles."

"More like a hundred miles." She backed off the anger immediately.

"Which doesn't mean much, since it's Texas miles, and there's not much civilization from here to there."

"Sorry. I didn't mean to get so—"

"Defensive?" he asked.

She tossed her jacket over the back of the couch and stashed her medical bag in the coat closet on the top shelf. "That's what we do to each other,

isn't it? Get defensive at first sight." She turned
to face him. "You were right earlier about not
fighting. I don't like being this way either, Cade.
It gets easy to do, like a habit, and I don't want
Michael seeing it."

"Then we'll have to make sure we don't."

"Agreed. No more fighting," she said, kicking off her shoes then dropping down into the
overstuffed chair near the stairs. Said with a sly
grin, "But clarify this for me, will you? Does the
ban on fighting include low blows, subtle innu-
endoes, and casual jabs? And this means both of
us, doesn't it? It's not like I have to quit fighting
with you, but you still get to fight with me, is it?"

Cade chuckled. "You always came out swinging with the best of them. We did have our good
moments, though, didn't we?"

"Enough that I could probably count them on
both hands."

"OK, I'm going to count that as a casual jab,
but it came damned close to being a low blow," he
warned her, smiling. "Which means you owe me."

"There's a penalty system connected to this
truce? Do I need to have my lawyers go over the

terms of the contract?" It was said with neither inflection nor expression.

"See, that's the thing. Most people would take what you said as a serious comment because you don't even crack a smile. But I know the sign, Belle."

"What sign?"

"The arched left eyebrow."

"I do not!" she said, feigning indignance.

"There it goes again, arching up, just for a split second. Subtle, but, oh, so readable."

"OK, so maybe I underestimated the number of good moments we had together. Does that get me off the hook for the penalty?"

"Eyebrow up again. And no. You're not off the hook."

"Try collecting," she challenged, shoving herself out of the chair and heading for the stairs.

This time it was Cade's turn to arch an eyebrow.

It wasn't the largest medical office, but it was modern—twenty years ago. Belle preferred to think of it as practical. She loved it, every last tongue depressor and cotton swab. She also loved the quaint little waiting room where noncommunicable patients sat nearly knee to knee, and the ten-year-old TV was permanently on the rerun channel. On a positive note, Belle did make sure the magazine subscriptions were up-to-date, and the coffee in the coffee-pot was refreshed every hour. Oh, and tea for the tea-drinkers. A couple of her old-timer patients had suggested that a little additive to the tea and coffee would be nice, and she'd assumed whiskey. But she hadn't dignified the hints with a response, and truly hoped her predecessor hadn't indulged in the practice.

Today was a busy day, and her receptionist, Ellen Anderson, another employee inherited along with the practice, was nearly frantic answering the phone, serving drinks, and sorting through patient charts for insurance billing information. In Big Badger, it seemed like people required medical attention in droves. One day they trickled in, the next day they flocked. She couldn't figure it out, and those she asked were pretty noncommittal on the subject. So this was a droves day, and Belle was ushering them in and out as fast as she could, given the nature of the various complaints.

"So, Mr. Biddle, you've had gout before?"

"Expect I did, Doctor. Some time last year, late in the spring, if I recall."

"And did Dr. Nelson give you any specific instructions on how to take care of yourself?" Emmett Biddle's gout was limited to his left big toe. "Diet, how much to drink, that sort of thing?"

"He did mention drinking water, I believe."

Polite man, age seventy-nine. Sharp. Still a cowboy. In fact, he'd ridden in on his horse today. Tied it to the hitching post, which happened to come along with the medical office. Impractical, she'd thought at first, but Emmett Biddle wasn't the first one to saddle up and come to an appointment on horseback. "And restrict or cut out your alcohol consumption?"

"Don't recall that, ma'am."

The twinkle in his eyes suggested otherwise. "Well, here's what I'd like you to do. Drink eight to sixteen cups of fluid each day—half that has to be water, and the other half cannot be alcohol. In fact, avoid alcohol. Or limit it to one small drink a day if you have to have it. Eat a moderate amount of protein, preferably from healthy sources, such as low-fat or fat-free dairy—" She would have said "tofu" next, but there was no way Emmett

Biddle was a tofu-eating kind of a man, so she skipped that. "Eggs and peanut butter are good, too. Also, limit your daily intake of meat, fish, and poultry to no more than six ounces."

"Six ounces is only one big bite of steak, ma'am. What am I going to survive on if I can't have my steak?"

"You can have it, just not as much."

"Sissy portions," Emmett grumbled as he slid off the table and picked up his cowboy boot, then bent down to tug it on. "Not fitting for a man to eat sissy portions."

"You should probably try soft shoes, too, like a pair of athletic shoes." Sandals worked, too, but she didn't see Emmett in sandals. Texas men don't wear sissy shoes, he'd probably tell her. "And here's a prescription for an anti-inflammatory. Follow the directions on the bottle—one pill a day, with food." But not steak, she wanted to say.

"It'll help with the pain? 'Cause it's getting so I can barely walk. And getting up on my horse is kind of hard nowadays, too."

"It will help, but if you don't follow my advice, you're going to keep on having trouble. And it could get worse." She scribbled something in the chart, then opened the exam-room door. "I want to see you back here in two weeks. I'll have another prescription for something you can take long term to help prevent the flare-ups. But nutrition, Mr. Biddle, plays an important part in controlling your gout."

"My nutrition is fine, young lady. It's kept me healthy seventy-nine years, with an occasional cold, and I'm not changing it for a toe ache."

She hadn't thought he would. Didn't really blame him either. At his age Emmett deserved to do what he wanted. "Two weeks, Mr. Biddle. Don't forget to make an appointment."

She wasn't sure what kind of noise he made on his way out, something between a grunt and a snort, but with a very clear message that she probably wouldn't be seeing Emmett Biddle, once the medication worked, until his next flare-up.

"Gout?" Cade questioned. He was standing in the doorway to her private office, taking up most of the space within it.

An imposing figure of a man, Belle thought as she stopped short of squeezing by him. "Patient confidentiality," she responded. "What do you want, Cade?"

He shrugged. "Just passing time until Michael's out of school. Thought I'd stop by and see if you needed any help."

"As in helping as a doctor?" Judging by his eyes, he seemed sincere enough. But Cade came within a hair's breadth of loathing general practice. At least, he used to. "Is that what you're offering?" she asked, not sure what to expect.

"If you need it. No pressure, though, Belle. I know this is your practice, and I'm sure you run it the way you see fit, but if you need help while I'm here—sure. I can do that when I'm not with Michael."

That was a surprise. Cade seemed almost humble. Something new, in her experience. Admittedly, part of the initial Cade Carter charm had been his cockiness. She'd been attracted. But life had changed, their situations had changed, and his old cockiness didn't work for her the way it once had. After she'd had Michael, she'd needed mellow and supportive. Almost what she was seeing now in Cade. "Well, I'm pretty busy most of the time. Between my practice and taking care of a number of ranches—house calls—it keeps me moving.

But can you handle what you used to call mundane work, like gout?"

"Then it *was* gout. I thought so, by the way he limped."

"That diagnosis coming from a surgeon?"

"We surgeons do come into contact with other medical problems from time to time."

"And you surgeons, according to the surgeon I used to be married to, don't particularly care to deal with anything non-surgical." She took a step closer, taking care not to get too close. "So can you really handle this, Cade? Because I could use help. But I don't want it to become an issue between us, since we already have enough of those going on."

"How about split the work? You get more time with Michael, I still get my time with Michael. We all win. It's not an issue, Belle."

"Do you have cowboy boots with you?" He'd had them back in Chicago. He'd always joked something about taking the cowboy out of Texas but not taking Texas out of the cowboy. Suddenly she could picture those boots paired with some nice tight jeans and a T-shirt that hugged his abs.

Rugged. All man. Probably not the way she should be thinking about her ex, though. Still...

"I never come to Texas without them."

She smiled. "Well, go and put them on and I'll put you to work."

"The cowboy look. Is that for you, or for—?"

"For image, Cade. That's all. Just for the image. Now move. I need to get into my office."

With that, he tipped his imaginary hat, then stepped aside. "I don't suppose you've ever given in to the boots, have you?"

Instead of answering, Belle simply shook her head. "When you get back, I'll have three patients for you. Then we're going to take a ride out to Ruda del Monte. We've got about a dozen hands there, with a few assorted other employees, and I have a contract to do physical exams on all of them. Thought maybe now that I have help, we could get started this afternoon." She smiled. "You still up for it, Cade?"

"See you in twenty minutes, Belle," he said, then spun around and swaggered away.

She couldn't help watching that swagger until it turned the corner and disappeared. So, what was she doing, letting Cade work with her? It was crazy. She had huge misgivings. But she also had a modest case of tingles. And that's what worried her the most. Especially as, for the past five years, she'd been under the impression she was impervious.

"What a nice young man, that Doc Cade is," Mrs. Kitty Peabody commented as she stepped into the hall, preparing to leave the office. "I'm glad someone's come to work with you. You needed the help. So is he your boss, dear?" she asked, blinking innocently as she looked up at Belle.

Belle bit the inside of her lips, trying hard to plaster some facsimile of a smile to her face. "No, he's not my boss. He's my—" No need to air the dirty family laundry. "He's my temp. He's in town on business for the next few weeks, and he needed a place to work, so I took him in."

"That's a casual jab, if ever I've heard one," Cade whispered in Belle's ear as he stepped up behind her. He turned to Mrs. Peabody. "We were married to each other, years ago. She had a hard time getting over me."

"Definitely a low blow," Belle said, out of the corner of her mouth.

"I can see why she would," Mrs. Peabody said to Cade. "If I were fifty years younger…"

Cade stepped forward and wrapped his arm around the woman's shoulder. "If you were fifty years younger, I'd be sitting on your front-porch swing right now—you do have a front-porch swing, don't you, Mrs. Peabody?"

The old woman raised her fingertips to her lips and giggled. "No, but if you want to come visit, I'll have my grandson hang one."

"You tell me when it's up, and I'll be the one to take the maiden swing." He shot a free and easy wink in Belle's direction as he escorted the woman to the reception area, while Belle stood there, staring, amazed.

"Who are you?" she asked a minute later when Cade came ambling back down the hallway. "And what did you do with Cade Michael Carter?"

"I'm simply a doctor who's trying to get along with his partner."

"Except I'm not your partner, Cade."

"That's right. I'm your temp, the one who showed up on your doorstep, begging for work."

Said with the biggest, brightest grin she'd seen since she'd, well, divorced him. "You're different," she commented, moving past him, on her way into the exam room to look after three-year-old Bonnie Thompson, a little girl who was prone to getting hives.

"In a good way?" he asked.

"Guess time will tell," she said, grabbing Bonnie's chart from the rack on the door then stepping into the exam room. Once inside, it took her a full ten seconds to find her focus before she turned into a doctor again. "So, Mrs. Thompson, did you make that list of foods, soaps, and things Bonnie commonly comes in contact with, and when, then note the time of her outbreaks?"

The girl's mother shrugged. "That takes a lot of time, Doctor. I have three other children, and my husband is on the road half the time. I wanted to. Even bought a notebook, and started, but…"

She held the notebook out for Belle to see. First page, marked day one. No entry other than oatmeal, orange juice. Not much to go on. "Does Bonnie drink orange juice every day?" she asked, picking up the child's arm to look at the red welts popping up below her elbow.

"Yes. In the morning. She loves it!"

"Bonnie," Belle said, "will you pull up your shirt so I can look at your tummy?"

Bonnie obliged quickly, and Belle found exactly what she expected to find. More welts. The same with the child's back and bottom. Not severe, not infected. But definitely hives that seemed to come and go at will. "For now, keep her off orange juice. And I know I've asked you to switch detergents, but this time I want you to double-wash Bonnie's clothes separately, first in a detergent without fragrance or brighteners, then the second time in clear water."

"Did I mention that I have three other children to take care of?" the woman asked, almost irately.

"You did, and I sympathize. But unless you want Bonnie to keep itching, we're going to have to get aggressive about finding out what's causing her allergy."

"Dr. Nelson gave her pills," Mrs. Thompson replied.

"And I've prescribed medication as well. But she can't go on taking it forever. So I want to find the cause of the problem so we can avoid it altogether."

"What about some kind of test? Wouldn't that be better than guessing?"

Guessing often played a part in medical diagnosis but Mrs. Thompson didn't want to hear that. Of course, Belle hadn't wanted to hear guesses either when Michael had been undergoing his diagnosis. "The tests are expensive, Mrs. Thompson, and unless something has changed, you have no medical insurance. If you want to pay out of pocket, that's fine. I'll have Ellen schedule an appointment with an allergist. Or you can do it the way I've suggested, which may take a little longer but in most cases can give us the same diagnosis." In the meantime, she didn't have time to waste arguing with a mother who didn't want the inconvenience of a little extra effort. It angered Belle. Really, truly angered her. Because if there was such an easy, simple fix for Michael, she'd be all over it in a second. No questions, no resentments, no holding back. But hives and Asperger's were two entirely different things and, in most cases, hives could be cured.

"Why the scowl?" Cade asked, as he hung up his borrowed white coat.

Belle shrugged. "I guess I don't get it some-times. One of my patients, a little girl with an un-specified allergy, is getting hives. She's not sick, they're not causing her any problems, and I'm keeping them under control with a couple of dif-ferent meds. But her mother—"

"Let me guess. Not a mother-of-the-year can-didate."

"She's a good mother, but she doesn't do enough. Seems put out when I give her suggestions. Wants an easier way out."

"In other words, not up to your mothering stan-dards?"

"I'm not an über-mom, if that's what you're getting at." She handed her last patient chart to Ellen to file away, then picked up her medical bag, ready to hit the road. "But if there was something I could give to Michael to fix the problems he has, I'd move heaven and earth to give it a try."

"I know you would," Cade said, donning his cowboy hat then tipping the brim at Maudie, who practically melted when he followed it up with a wink. "But trust me. Not all mothers have that higher purpose. There are some mothers who weren't meant to be. One of nature's practical jokes, I think. But you're the kind of mother every child should have." Said in all sincerity. "The kind I wish..." His voice trailed off, and he ended the sentence with a sigh.

"Your flattery scares me, Cade," Belle said, wondering where that comment had come from. And that sigh, as well as the look in Cade's eyes when he'd made it—did she see sadness there?

"Then you're out of practice," Maudie quipped, breaking up the serious moment and clearly aligning with Cade as she scooted by on her way to the supply closet. "Because most people would be pleased with a compliment from someone like Dr. Carter."

"Cade, please," Cade said. "No need to stand on formalities here."

For the second time Maudie almost melted. Her normally steely eyes turned mushy, and her thin lips unfolded into a generous smile. In fact, she was so smitten with the man she was nearly batting her eyelashes at him. Quite unlike anything Belle had ever witnessed in her office nurse until Cade. Now she was concerned. More than that, she was suspicious. What in the world was Cade up to, ingratiating himself that way in a place he didn't need to ingratiate himself?

It made her wonder. Made her think. But at the end of it all she still didn't know. And that made her worry.

CHAPTER THREE

"How many miles do you travel, on average?" Cade asked, settling back into the passenger's seat of Belle's beat-up car. Old model, lots of dents and rust. It was a constant source of irritation to him since he'd been offering to buy her a new vehicle for the past two years. But she was as stubborn as she was pretty, and there was no budging on her refusal. She would buy another vehicle when she could afford to pay for it herself. And she was always quick to tell him that beat-up didn't mean it wasn't dependable. Well, in spite of her bull-headed refusal, he kept the option open to her, because of Michael.

"My farthest ranch is the Chachalaca, which is a hundred-mile round trip. Today we're only going out about twenty-five miles."

"Hope they pay you for the inconvenience," he said, tipping his black cowboy hat down over his eyes.

"I'm paid adequately, not that it's any of your business."

"Enough to get you better wheels? Because I'm still concerned about that, Belle. For you, for Michael, when he's with you. You need something better than this bucket of rust."

"This bucket of rust is fine. I had the mechanic check it a couple weeks ago when I put on new tires, and he said other than the fact that it doesn't look good, it's OK. So don't try the emotional blackmail stunt by dragging Michael into this, because it's not going to work. There's nothing wrong with my car, and Michael's perfectly safe riding in it."

"Until it stalls out in the middle of nowhere and you've got to contend not only with a stalled car but with Michael's anxieties. And you know that's going to happen, Belle. Maybe not this week, or even next month, but eventually the car's going to die a gruesome death and I sure as hell don't want my son in it when it does."

"Your son? Did you forget that he's my son, too?"

"Actually, that's probably the thing I've been thinking about most lately. How he's your son, but he never quite makes it over to being my son." He didn't resent Belle, but he'd been spending too many sleepless nights lately, trying to figure out what to do. Pacing the floor. Standing, staring out the window, sometimes for an hour or more, lost in his thoughts. Going out for middle-of-the-night walks, hoping to exhaust himself. Making unnecessary night rounds on his surgical patients in the hospital simply to occupy time. Unfortunately, his efforts never got him any answers, and they didn't help him sleep. In fact, the harder he tried to find those answers, the more confused he became.

"It's not the way I want it, Cade. It's just the way it is—right now. But Michael will change. It takes time."

"I know that. But it's frustrating coming down here twice a month and seeing how everything is exactly the same as it was the last time I visited, and the time before that. Which means I simply have to accept the situation for what it is, or try harder. Or differently. And I know that. So I'll quit bugging you about your car when I quit worrying, which won't be until after you have better wheels under you. At least give me that much satisfaction."

She laughed. "You want satisfaction? OK, once a week. But that's all you're getting from me. You can bug me about my car once a week. And as far as Michael goes, I like the idea of trying differently. I do that, all the time. Every day, in fact. And sometimes I see these amazing advances, then sometimes I see—well, nothing. But Michael's very open to new things, even though he might not show it the way you'd expect. Also, it may take him a little longer to fit them into his normal routine, yet once he does, he can become very enthusiastic if it's something he enjoys. So maybe, instead of trying to fit yourself into his regular niche differently, you should think about creating one that's just for the two of you. You know, develop something new where Michael has to depend on you for guidance."

Turning the corner, they headed off the main highway down a dirt road where the next twenty miles of scenery could only be described as bare, with an occasional clump of sagebrush. He loved Texas, even with its sparse scenery. It had an honesty that made sense to him. Maybe that's why he loved it. Probably why he missed it, too. But he'd never considered coming back on a permanent basis. Too many painful memories to deal with. Too many unhappy things he didn't want to look back on in his life.

Yet Michael was here, so every other week, rain or shine, hell or high water, he packed an overnight bag, hopped a plane, and here is where he landed, regrets and all. Here as in Texas, not here as in sitting next to Belle—and a nice sitting it was, he did have to admit. Somehow, over the years, he'd forgotten how absolutely wonderful she smelled, like flowers and sunshine. He missed that, actually. Missed a lot about her, and while they shared custody, the obligatory parental handoff when he came to get Michael rarely involved her in any substantial way. Oh, she'd greet him at the door, be cordial—hardly ever let him into her house, though. And words between them were few and far between unless there was something to discuss about their son.

Other than that, he didn't know what was going on in her life. Did she have good friends in Big Badger? Or a serious relationship? Did she even date, or was she reclusive? Was she happy now?

Cade tried picturing her with someone other than him—maybe this Dr. Robinson she thought so highly of. Had the personal support this Dr. Robinson gave Belle turned into something more? He thought about it for a moment, wasn't sure how he felt about it. "So, what would your Dr. Robinson suggest I might try with Michael?" he asked, still trying to picture the guy, hoping to God that Robinson was grandfatherly and not someone with the abs Belle seemed to like.

"Honestly, I don't know. Maybe something not even remotely close to anything he does, or likes now."

"Maybe I should talk to him myself, see what he suggests."

"Who, Michael?"

"No. Dr. Robinson."

A strange smile crept to Belle's lips. "First thing, Dr. Robinson is a great advocate of making the discoveries yourself. The merit in that is the journey. And second thing, Dr. Robinson's first name is Amanda."

Cade smiled uncomfortably. OK, so maybe he had that one coming. Still, he did wonder about Belle's social life. Especially certain aspects of it. After all, any man connected to Belle would be connected to his son, so that made it his right to know. At least, that's what he was telling himself and, halfway, trying to believe. "So, what kind of new interest do you think Michael might enjoy? Something athletic? I've never had the impression he likes sports very much." Not the best recovery from his almost-gaffe, but the only one he could come up with. Had Belle seen through what might have looked like a little bit of jealousy? Even though that's not what he'd really intended, that little smile on her lips caused him to blush.

"Did you just want to come right out and ask me?"

"What?" he asked, even though he knew exactly what.

"If I'm involved with anybody."

"If it affects Michael, I'd have the right to know."

"Maybe you would, maybe you wouldn't." Her smile broadened. "But I suppose you'll never know if you don't ask the question."

"What if I just said that I trust you to make the right decisions about the people you bring into Michael's life?"

"Not good enough, Cade. You're dying to ask. Admit it."

"I'm curious, yes."

"Curious enough to just ask me if I'm involved?"

"Are you?"

"See. That wasn't so bad, was it?"

"It won't be once you tell me, so we can end this conversation." She was enjoying this, enjoying seeing him squirm. Being pretty bold about it, too. Part of that straightforwardness he usually liked but was finding a little vexing at the moment.

"OK, no. Nobody. Not involved. No time. Not even sure there's anyone in Big Badger who would be my type."

"And your type would be…?"

"You were, once. Don't know any more. So anyway," she continued without missing a beat, "Michael likes soccer. Plays on the junior league at school. Started off as a midfielder, then they moved him to goalie because he has incredible focus on the ball—never loses sight of it. Oh, and he likes horseback riding, too, when I have the time to take him…which isn't often enough. And hiking. One of his favorite things in the world is hiking out into the wilderness and just—well, I guess the best way to describe it is observe the things around him. Michael has this uncanny eye for spotting things nobody else would even notice."

Well, now he knew about her relationship status. Wasn't sure how he felt about it one way or another, but at least he knew. "I knew someone like that once. He could sit and watch a bug for hours. Or the movement of leaves in the wind. The smallest details fascinated him. There was this one time when he was watching this cloud formation…" He stopped, swallowed hard, regrouped. "Why haven't you told me any of these things about my—our—son?"

"You never asked. Since you are now, I think your visits with him have gotten into a bit of a routine—go get pizza, get ice cream, go see a movie, play video games. And I'm not faulting you for that, Cade. But don't blame me for you not getting to know what your son likes. All you had to do was ask me, or ask Michael. He might not tell you the first time, or even the tenth time, but eventually he would tell you. For that matter, have you ever asked him what he wants to do when you visit? He will have opinions, but he's not going to come right out and say them."

Cade exhaled a deep breath. She was right, of

course, every single, frustrating, insightful word she said. Which pointed out how miserably he failed at the thing that meant the most to him— being a dad. Well, he had six weeks to work on it, six weeks to change things or, at least, make the situation better. And six weeks where pizza, ice cream, movies and video games weren't going to be enough. "I think I have an idea," he said. "Not sure it would work, but—"

"Sometimes, Cade," Belle interrupted, "it's not so much about what you do with him as it is the fact that you're with him. That's what's important, and I think Michael would probably enjoy quality time over all your trivial pursuits. And I'm not faulting you for those. I know it's tough being a part-time parent."

Suddenly, his anger flared. His back went rigid. He tipped his hat off his face for a direct confrontation. "I'm never a part-time parent, Belle. When you still lived in Chicago, I bought a condo one block from your apartment to make sure I could see Michael, and stay involved with him as much as possible. But you're the one who took my son and moved over a thousand miles away. You're the one who took away my involvement, who limited me. But that doesn't make me a part-time parent, because I'm his father twenty-four hours a day. The father, by the way, who was never told that his son was a hell of a soccer goalie."

"When was the last time you asked me what Michael was involved in, Cade? You come here, spend your weekends trying to do your best with him, and I know you're angry because it doesn't always work out the way you want it to, or the way you think it should, but…" She shook her head fiercely. "Don't blame me for moving. I have a life, too. Something that you never seemed to recognize when we were married—where my time was soon taken up with caring for a house, a husband, and a baby. I had to let opportunities pass me by but then I got my shot, Cade, and it was here. I'm sorry you don't get enough time with Michael because of that, but that's the way it worked out. We live here now, this is our home, and Michael's adjusting. And if I forgot to mention that our son is one hell of a goalie, or that he's pretty good on the back of a horse, maybe it's because I'm the only doctor within a hundred miles, I'm on call every hour of every day of the week, I have custodial care of our son and manage to be a pretty involved mom, and I get by on four hours of sleep a night, if I'm lucky. And this isn't arguing, by the way. It's me expressing my point of view in an exasperated manner."

Damn, this wasn't the way he'd wanted it to go. What he'd thought he was getting into when he committed himself to spending the next six weeks here, well, he wasn't sure. Maybe as little as trying to make peace with Belle, again. All the way down here he kept telling himself it was for Michael's sake. But one look at her, and he knew it was for his sake as well. They shared a son. They shouldn't be fighting or expressing exasperated points of view. But put them together in the same room, the same car, even the same town, and that's what happened. They came out swinging. There were huge emotions involved. Yet he didn't believe there was any hatred mixed in there. Had never believed it. More like it was a breakdown of everything they'd once believed in. A flame had died out. "I know it's tough, and I'm sorry. And you're welcome to your exasperated point of view, but I'm entitled to mine as well. OK?"

"OK," she said, backing off the raging heat of

the moment. "And I know I get a little defensive—mostly with you."

He chuckled. "We always did have a way with bringing out the worst in each other, didn't we?"

"And the best, sometimes."

"Sometimes…" Cade sighed, relaxing back into the seat. Sometimes had been pretty great, but it was difficult wading through the rest of it to find the good. "Not enough times, though. That was our problem, I think. The best was awesome, but we couldn't find it often enough. And I'm not blaming you, Belle. You tried, and I didn't."

"It takes two, Cade. Either way it goes, it takes two." She glanced over at him, simply studied him for a fraction of a second, then laughed. "But if you want to own most of the responsibility for our breakdown, that's OK with me."

She turned her attention back to the dirt road and the never-ending expanse of nothingness stretching out in front of them. But in that fraction of a second when she'd looked at him, he'd felt…there weren't any words to describe it, really, except she'd looked not into his soul but through it, and it shook him. Shook him badly. "OK with me, too," he conceded. But seriously. "For our son.

Because I really want to make this work, Belle. We may not be married, but Michael needs consistency from us, together. You know. A united front."

"He needs us to be the adults, you mean?"

"The adults. And there was a time when those adults in question could actually stand to be in the same room together."

"I can stand being in the room with you, Cade. And that's not just about Michael."

He was surprised to hear that. So surprised, in fact, that he tilted his hat down, almost covering his whole face, and smiled the rest of the way to Ruda del Monte.

"So how many of these physicals do we have to do?" he asked, reaching into the back seat to grab a medical bag.

"Twenty. With the *E. coli* outbreak over at the Chachalaca, I've had several calls from other ranch managers who are worried about their hands. Ruda del Monte is actually the first ranch that's doing something about it pre-emptively, but I have an idea that within the week I'll have another five or six ranches join in. Especially if we see symptoms popping up anywhere else."

"This *E. coli*, it's spreading?" He slammed shut the car door and walked around to the driver's side, and waited there while Belle grabbed her medical bag and shrugged into her white coat—something he thought looked totally out of place, given the circumstances. But, then, so did her tan linen slacks, her blue silk blouse, and her string of pearls. Damn, if she didn't look good but, damn, if she didn't look out of place on a working ranch. His first instinct was that he was going to have to teach her the finer points of Texas style, but his second instinct reminded him she wasn't his to teach. Sometimes it was hard remembering those distinctions. "Any symptoms in town?"

"A few. The county health officials told me it was salad ingredients, and I took their word for it. Our grocery supplier here also supplies a number of the ranches, so that makes sense. But the thing is, the outbreak isn't widespread, so..."

"So you're wondering, what?" he asked, falling into step with her.

She shrugged. "Why is it contained when everybody's eating from the same source? Shouldn't there be more people sick? Anyway, the county health department is testing for it, which means for now the only thing we can do is treat the people when they're sick. So far, we've been lucky. All the symptoms I've seen have been mild."

He thought about it for a moment. As a surgeon, this was totally out of his league, but he did recall outbreaks known to have been caused by broccoli, lettuce, bean sprouts. So the salad theory made sense. Except Belle wasn't convinced, and if there was one thing about Belle he knew beyond a doubt, she was one hell of a doctor. More than that, she had the finest instinct he'd ever seen in medicine. So if she didn't believe it was the salad, neither did he. "Then the physicals are just cursory?"

She nodded. "Maybe. I have an idea there may be more to it since there was some urgency to the call. But the foreman denied anything was wrong with any of his hands, so until I know differently I'm going to have to take him at his word. Right now, I'm going to take a basic look, ask some questions." Smiling, "Earn my monthly retainer."

"Oh, I guess I didn't realize you're getting into concierge medicine out here." Payment meant to keep a doctor on retainer, much like many corporations paid to keep their lawyers on retainer, whether or not they used their professional services.

"I guess you could call it that. I prefer to think of it as the smartest way to recruit a good doctor. And before you ask, all the ranches have me on retainer. And they're honoring my terms, because I'm saving to buy the medical practice from the town, to make it my own. The town bought it from Doc Nelson when he needed the money for his new life—a young wife and a beach condo can get pretty expensive, I hear. Anyway, the town's made it perfectly clear they don't want to be in the medicine business for long, so the practice is mine to buy back from the town if I want it. And I do, because I need permanent roots for Michael and me, a real home, and it's going to be in Big Badger. So my goal is to have the practice bought and paid for inside three years."

Cade shook his head, whistled a low whistle. "That's going to take some effort."

"You don't think I can do it?"

"Quite the opposite. But I guess I thought you'd get over it and eventually come back to Chicago."

"Get over what? My need to be independent?"

"Your need to stay as far away from me as possible."

Rather than getting angry, Belle laughed out loud. "You're really full of yourself, do you know that? My coming here has nothing to do with you and everything to do with me." She pointed in the direction of the side door. "And so you'll know, you were as insignificant to me in Chicago as you are to me here." Then, she smiled sweetly. "Getting more so every day."

"Remember those last few miserable months of marriage, when we were both consumed with trying to figure out what we were going to do?"

"Definitely miserable months."

He cocked an amused eyebrow. "You didn't have to agree so quickly."

"What's true is true, though."

He pondered that for a moment, shrugged, then grinned. "Anyway, I was trying hard to figure out what I ever saw in you in the first place."

"That's harsh."

"What's true is true, though," he mimicked. "And I finally remembered. You were incredible, Belle. Smart, funny, with a barbed tongue that could slit you open at a hundred paces..."

"I'll take that as a compliment," she said, bending slightly at the waist to bow to him. "Whether or not you meant it as one."

"Oh, I meant it to be a compliment. One of the things I loved most about you was your sharp wit. You always had an answer for everything, and God pity the person who crossed you, because your answers could get lethal. Sometimes I liked to stand back and watch you in action."

"When you say in action, I'm assuming you mean something to do with my sharp wit and my lethal answers." She met his stare directly, and challenged it head-on. "That's what you liked?"

Damn, she was sexy when she stared at him that way. Someone else might have found it intimidating, but he found it to be another of the things he missed about Belle. It was a growing list, one he was surprised he had in him. Close proximity, he decided. And maybe a little unfinished business between them. That's all it could be. "Did back then. Still do." Too bad they weren't able to stay focused on the good things, but those last months had turned into a nightmare. She had been justifiably angry, he had been unjustifiably defensive. Not some of his finest moments, and he didn't like thinking about that time in his life—their lives. So he jumped straight into safe territory. "Before we go in, how do we divide up our patients here? Or do we?"

"Well, if this place turns out to be like the Chachalaca, we won't have to worry about dividing anything. They'll flock to you. Probably trample everybody in their way getting out of my line to go and stand in yours."

"Yet you want to settle here?"

She shrugged. "They'll get used to me—in ten or twenty years." That last was said almost under her breath.

"Well, if you want to endear yourself, lose the pearls and the silk blouse. Buy yourself a good pair of boots, some nice, tight-fitting jeans and a T-shirt, maybe even a hat like mine." He tipped the brim up for her. "Try to fit in, not set yourself apart. It'll go a long way." OK, so he hadn't meant to get involved, but he couldn't help himself. It was Belle after all. And while she wasn't exactly in over her head, she was up to her neck and didn't even know it. Besides, it was only advice. In the truest Belle Carter fashion, she'd probably ignore it anyway.

"And you know this because…"

"Because I was born and raised in Texas. I'm one of them."

"Yet you married a woman who wore silk and pearls."

"Temporarily lost my way." Blinded by love for a little while. "But I got over it." Not as much as he'd thought, he was fast discovering.

"Want to know one of the things I miss most about you?" she asked, on her way to the door.

"What?"

She didn't answer. Instead, she opened the door, walked through, and shut it in his face.

"Well, damn!" he said, smiling.

"Anything unusual?" she asked Cade an hour later.

"Two with mild symptoms, like you suspected." He handed her the notes he'd made. "And one with a problem of a personal nature."

"Personal nature."

He wiggled mischievous eyebrows at her. "Let's

just say that I prescribed him an enhancement medication, and leave it at that."

"I did a thorough physical on every one of these men a month ago, and nobody…" She stopped, nodded. "Because I'm a woman first, then a doctor. At least, to them."

"It's a man thing, so don't take it personally."

"If I had time, I might. But I've also got two with symptoms, and another one who's laid up in the bunkhouse, not able to come down here to the ranch office. He's telling the manager there's nothing wrong with him as he bends over in knots with cramps. And to be honest about this, I'm getting a little concerned. After I get the test results back, I'm going to have maybe twenty confirmed cases of *E. coli* between the ranches and town, and this has only been going on for four days."

"But the common denominator is still the salad fixings. They had it for dinner a couple of days ago. I've got the cook rounding up samples to send to the lab… I'm assuming you'll want to send them to the lab. Or am I overstepping my bounds as a doctor?"

She smiled. "As a surgeon, you're brilliant. As a diagnostician and purveyor of sexual enhancement drugs, you're pretty good, too. And, yes, send it to the lab. I'm sending everything I can get my hands on right now. Oh, and look, Cade, for what it's worth, I'm glad you're here. We had our bad times, but I've always thought you were the best doctor I've ever seen."

"Except for you. That's what you're thinking, isn't it?"

She wrinkled her nose at him. "Of course that's what I'm thinking. Anyway, I'm on my way to the bunkhouse to see what we've got there."

"With the serious cramps, think *E.coli* could have resulted in hemolytic uremic syndrome?" A condition resulting from the abnormal destruction of red blood cells, known to clog the filtering system in the kidneys, which could lead to kidney failure, even death.

"Depends on a lot of factors. Especially his overall health. I'd given that some thought, but normally you don't see that kind of complication for eight to ten days after onset. You could be on to something, though. Maybe he got into the contaminant before the others did, or he has some kind of underlying condition that brought it on sooner." She picked up her pace on the way to the bunkhouse, pleased to see that Cade was going with her. Not that she couldn't handle this on her own, because she could. And she intended to, maybe even for the rest of her medical career. Still, he was nice to have around, even temporarily, and he did give her a little boost of confidence, which she'd never, ever let him know. "Don't know what we're looking for, but all my patient notes for everyone on the ranch are available right here." She held up her electronic pad.

"I'm impressed."

"Actually, so am I. It was Michael's suggestion. First day in the office, he looked at the old file system, hit a few computer keys and saw what we had available there, and told me I had to update if I wanted to be efficient. 'Mom, you've got to understand that good medicine is about the technology, too.'"

"That's what my son said?" he said, his voice full of pride.

"That's what our son said. So I hired a tech to come make changes. Michael wanted to do them himself, by the way."

"You didn't let him?"

"He's seven. He may have the capability, but he

needs to be seven, not an adult. Anyway, going electronic is a slow, ongoing process. But that's changing, and I now have, as they say, connectivity. So I'm uploading all my ranch files first." She pointed up to the sky. "My own link to a satellite that links to my computer that links to my patient files, or something like that."

"Amazing kid."

No arguments there. Michael was amazing, and it was time for his parents to be a little more amazing as well. "So, Mr. Ralston, can you tell me how you're feeling?" she asked. Even before she was all the way across the room to Dean Ralston's bedside, she knew the answer to her question. He was confused. It registered in his eyes. And he was pale. There were also small bruises around his nose and mouth. Face and hands swollen. All bad signs.

Without a word, she looked at Cade, who was already pulling out his cellphone. "Who do I call?" he whispered.

"We dispatch out of Laredo, which is a long way away. Why don't I do that while you take his vital signs? And I'll also go get an IV set up."

Within minutes she had a rescue helicopter

on its way, but its estimated time of arrival was something close to an hour, which didn't make her happy.

"Blood pressure's critical," Cade whispered when she came back to the bedside. "And unless I'm mistaken, I think he's had a stroke."

"Then you were right about the hemolytic uremic syndrome. It shouldn't have happened so soon, but it did."

"This man's an alcoholic, Belle." He opened the bottom compartment to Dean Ralston's bedside stand, to reveal a dozen or more mostly empty bottles of alcohol. "That's his underlying medical condition, and probably the reason this hit him so hard, so fast."

"The things we do to ourselves," she said, as she tried locating a good vein for an IV needle. Turned out that wasn't so easy. His veins were shot, she couldn't find a suitable site anywhere. "I think I'm going to have to go with a subclavian," she finally said. "Not my favorite thing to do."

"How about I go find something to jack up the end of the bed for you?" A measure to prevent the possibility of an air embolism.

"While you're at it, ask the foreman if Mr.

Ralston has anybody we should notify." She would have asked her patient, but he wasn't responsive at all. His eyes fluttered open, more a nerve twitch than anything else. For all intents and purposes, Dean Ralston was well on his way to slipping into a coma. And they'd told her it was stomach cramps! Well, they were wrong, and their aversion to calling a female doctor until it was almost too late for this poor man was going to be costly. "Mr. Ralston," she said, her voice deliberately loud, "I need to get an IV line in you. It's going to be up near your collarbone. We're also going to take you to the hospital in a few minutes. I believe you're having complications from some kind of food poisoning." Mild understatement. This man was critically ill and, given her limitations out here, she wasn't sure of his prognosis. Which now turned a mild *E. coli* outbreak into a serious one.

The next few minutes went textbook perfect. Cade, with the assistance of a couple of ranch hands, put the foot end of the bed up on bricks, while Belle placed a rolled towel between Ralston's shoulder blades to make his clavicles more prominent. Cade located the obvious landmarks for the IV insertion, while Belle anesthetized the area and swabbed it down with antiseptic. Then Cade inserted the IV line with the swift skill of a surgeon, while Belle attached the line to the bag. Cade readied a sterile dressing for the site, while Belle taped it into place. A perfect medical union, to anybody who cared to look. And all of it done without a spoken word between them, like they'd been working together as a cohesive team for years when, in fact, this was their very first time.

Thinking about how good they were together, good naturally, made her shiver. That's what concerned her when they readied their patient for transport to the hospital. It's what still concerned her when the helicopter lifted off. And concerned her even more an hour later, when she dropped Cade off at his boarding house. How could they be so perfectly in sync in a medical situation, but totally out of sync with everything else?

It didn't make sense. In all honesty, though, she didn't want it to. Cade needed to be an afterthought in her life. She'd finally put him in that place, and she wanted him to stay there. Problem was, that wasn't happening. In fact, if anything, this situation with him seemed to be going in the opposite direction.

"Not good," she was muttering two hours later, preparing grilled cheese sandwiches for the three of them as Cade had stopped by to visit with Michael.

"What's not good?" Cade asked, stepping up behind her. Dangerously close.

"The way I think I'm going to burn your sandwich."

"Burned by Belle Carter, could be interesting," he said, now pressed so close she could smell every drop of his potency.

She spun around to face him, and found herself caught in an impossible position—step forward into him, or backwards into the stove. Either way, she was the one who was about to get burned. Rather than allowing that to happen, Belle raised the spatula, shoved it at his chest, then sidestepped him. "Burned by Cade Carter, been there, done that." With that she walked with all the composure she could muster until she got up the stairs to her bedroom, where she locked the door behind her and gave way to wobbly knees that barely managed to carry her across the room to her bed.

Then, for the next ten minutes, she stared at the ceiling, too scared to think or breathe properly. Most of all, too scared to admit to herself that one step more and burned sandwiches would have been the least of her problems. The very least.

CHAPTER FOUR

"ONE night. That's all I'm asking for. Just one night to go camping with Michael, and it's not even going to be very far from here, Belle. Close enough that I can have him home in twenty minutes, if I have to."

"I guess my biggest concern is that he's never been camping." And she wasn't sure now was a good time to start. It took time to get Michael ready for new experiences, and while camping was something he might enjoy, at least she hoped he would, it was also something they shouldn't just spring on him. "Spontaneity isn't exactly part of Michael's comfort zone, Cade, and I haven't had time to, well, get him ready for camping. You know, like a trial run. Take him out into the wilderness for a couple hours, maybe two or three times, so he can get used to his surroundings. Spend a night in a tent in the back yard. He's very adaptable, and eager to learn new things, and also get involved in activities he's never done before, but at his own pace. You know, taking it deliberately." People singled that out as a characteristic of Asperger's, but she often wondered if it wouldn't be better if everybody slowed down a bit, and took life a little more deliberately. There was a time it had been called caution. Now it appeared on a list of traits used to identify a condition.

"One night is preparation. I'd like to take him out for a two- or three-day stretch at some point. Maybe even longer if he likes it. His choice, of course. But since you're so worried about doing it tonight, you could always come with us, if that would ease your mind."

Going camping with Cade and Michael? Maybe she was the one who needed the preparation time, because the thought of it made her uncomfortable. No, actually, it scared her to death. Spending a night in that kind of cozy proximity to Cade was a big part of that fear, owing to the way she'd felt all through their grilled cheese sandwiches the night before, as well as the fact that she'd never been camping in her life. Never slept outside, not even pretend camping in the back yard when she'd been a little girl. Then there was Michael's reaction, and who knew what that was going to be? OK, all of it gave her cause for worry, she'd admit it. But the thing that unsettled her the most was wondering why, after all these years, Cade was causing these strange feelings in her. It defied any explanation she could come up with. "How? I can't simply walk away from my practice. I'm the only—"

He held out his hand to stop her. "You have connectivity, remember? And like I said, we're not going far. Just out to the Ruda del Monte. There's an amazing area out in the back acreage and the owner, Jake Gibbons—who's a real nice guy— appreciates the way you take care of his ranch hands. Anyway, Jake gave me permission to use it any time I want."

"Just like that, he gave you permission?" How did Cade charm everybody in his path? Jake Gibbons was a grouch. An unadulterated, dyed-in-the-wool grouch, who had flat-out told her he didn't like the idea of a woman doctoring his men. Yet Cade had called him a real nice guy.

"Yep. Open-ended permission, and he said if I need supplies, to stop by and ask his foreman. So we're set for about everything a camper could want. And if any emergencies come up, you can come right back to town," he continued. "Besides that, I gave Maudie a set of walkie-talkies, just for more connectivity." He shrugged. "She's already agreed to take the call for anything minor that comes in."

"First Jake Gibbons, then you sweet-talked my nurse?" The charmed-by-Cade list was growing. Sure, he'd amazed her with that charm all those years ago when they'd met, and if she was still amazed by its effect, which she wasn't admitting to, she might be a little miffed that he succeeded where she, well—she wouldn't call it failed so much as stalled.

"She's a pushover."

"Because you flirted with her."

He grinned. Tilted his hat back and arched wickedly sexy eyebrows at her. "Because I asked her. And smiled when I did it. She told me you never smile, Belle. So I suggested that you might come back smiling after a night of camping with your son. It could go a long way in your relationship with…everybody." He shrugged. "And Maudie sure seemed supportive to me. Very nice, too."

OK, so she was a little miffed. Why deny it?

After trying for two months to fit in here, without success, Cade had waltzed right in and done it immediately. One smile, one smooth word, and everybody loved him. While her they merely tolerated. The thing was, Belle was more than miffed, she was envious. Having that kind of rapport with people, she couldn't even imagine what it would be like. Dr. Cade Carter, he's the nice one. And Dr. Belle Carter, she's the serious one. Search a list of synonyms for serious and you got grave, persevering, severe, somber, even unplayful. Unplayful! She'd actually heard people say these things about her, though. And not just once or twice. "Well, supportive or not, we can't go camping, Cade. Don't you understand? Michael and I don't get to do things on the spur of the moment like other people do."

"But have you tried lately? He's growing up, Belle. His interests are changing, he's taking on new challenges. You have to allow him room for all that growth or at least give him the opportunity to see how it works. Then let him succeed or fail on his own, without you trying to shelter him from everything."

"I do allow him room. It's just that…" She exhaled a frustrated breath. Cade's view of the world was always rosy, always give it a try and it will work out, while she was practical or pragmatic. That was probably the biggest difference between them, the one that had rendered the final split. There were times when she'd have loved living in Cade's world, sharing his rose-colored glasses, believing that things would work out simply because you wanted them to, but reality always superseded. Yet who was she to deny Cade his tinted outlook, or Michael his opportunity to prove her wrong on so many levels? So it was off to camp with the two of them and, for Michael's sake, even for Cade's, she hoped this camp-out succeeded.

More than that, she wanted it to be fun for them. Michael deserved that with his father, and while she didn't care so much about what Cade deserved, there was still a part of her that believed he deserved that with his son. "OK, I'll ask him. But you'll have to abide by his decision. That's the best I can do."

"Then I'm going to ask you again. Come with us, Belle. The three of us, camping together. Maybe we're not the family we used to be, but we can make it work for one night. Otherwise you're going to be miserable, wondering what's happening. You'll stay up all night, pacing the floor." He winked. "Probably come sneaking out to the camp at three in the morning to make sure everything's fine. Then pace some more when you get home. So why not skip all the intermediary steps, pack an overnight bag, and come with us? It's already arranged."

Yes, it was arranged. But she didn't always trust Cade's arrangements. That suspicion sprang from years of his arrangements when they'd been married. *I'll only be gone a week. I'll call you every day. I promise I'll stay home for a while.* Yes, she was aware of his arrangements, and they didn't always work out. In fact, they didn't work out most of the time. "Then what I'm assuming is that you want me there so you can prove me wrong, and I can see it firsthand."

"You are wrong," he said, his voice so gentle it was barely more than a whisper. "But not about the things you think I think."

His voice, the way it was so quiet, so seductive, gave her goose-bumps. Always did. She rubbed her arms, trying to get rid of the chill, hoping he didn't notice. "You, um…you don't get to make

assumptions, Cade." She was fighting to stay focused on the camping trip, not on the way Cade
could still affect her simply by the way he spoke.
"That's what killed us in the first place. You assumed everything would work out, then left me
there alone to make it happen while you went off
and did whatever you wanted. And you took me
for granted, almost every day of our married life,
because there were things that needed to be fixed,
things I couldn't fix alone, that you assumed I
would, or could." OK, now she was back in the
moment. Past Cade's effect and on to the issues
at hand. Belle drew in a ragged breath, fighting
not to get angry. There had been enough of that
in the past, and she was a different person now.
She hoped Cade was, too, but she didn't really
know yet. "Look, I know you love Michael, and
I know that relationship is difficult for you. But
you're here to work it out with your son, not with
your ex-wife. So spare me the assumptions and
we'll get along fine. And while you're at it, don't
make plans for me again, then proceed to the arrangements and assume I'll be fine with it. I'm
not. Not on any level."

"You've changed," he said.

"I had to, if I wanted to survive. It's what you caused." And in many ways she was grateful, because she was better for it. But getting to this point had been so hard.

"Well, I don't know how to respond to that."

"You don't have to. I'm living the life I want, I'm happy. That it came about as a result of our divorce is unfortunate, because it would have been nice having the things I wanted inside our marriage. But none of that matters now. You're here because of Michael, and that's all there is between us—our son. Nothing else, Cade. Nothing else." But was that really true? Last week she'd have said an unequivocal yes. Today she wondered.

"Well, since this is about our son, I think he'd probably like to have his mother go camping with him. And that's not an assumption. Just a guess."

"But the question is, would his mother like to go camping?"

"I'll take care of you, Belle, if that's what you're worried about."

"Even though you know I'm not the outdoors type?"

"Because I know you're not the outdoors type."

It could work. She didn't take Friday afternoon

office calls, all of her ranch work was caught up, paperwork was completed. And she was available for emergencies certainly. Still, she cleared Friday afternoons to spend with Michael—a trip to the park, or the library, or maybe the movies. What they did was always Michael's choice, and that was as spontaneous as their lives ever got. So camping?

"Look, Belle. For what it's worth, and not to make you angry, but you're the one who seems to have a problem with spontaneity, so why don't you simply ask him if he wants to go camping, like you said you would, and go from there? One step at a time. And if this is about you and me camping together, I'll respect the distance, keep to my side of the line, whatever you want. For Michael."

He was trying. She couldn't fault Cade there. He was being everything he should be. "Fine, I'll talk to him on the way home from school, and see what he wants to do. Then I'll decide what I want to do after that."

"How about we talk to him?"

Another thing to worry about, since Michael wasn't quite responsive to Cade. But Cade was insistent, it was also his right as Michael's father, so she agreed. Reluctantly, though. And thirty minutes later Cade and Belle stood outside the main entrance to Big Badger Elementary, waiting for their son to come out, while inside, Michael looked out the window at the two of them huddled together, talking, and smiled a smile they didn't see.

"So that's what I'd like to do this afternoon and tonight," Cade said to Michael, who was fidgeting with his backpack while Belle paced in circles around the picnic table on the school playground. "I used to camp when I was a kid. Haven't done it in a long time, but I think we can have fun. So do you want to go?" Thus far, Michael hadn't done so much as glance at him, and Cade truly didn't know if he was even listening. "You know, give it a try, see if you like it?" Then when Michael responded with a single nod of his head, Cade wasn't sure what to make of it. "Is that a yes?"

Michael nodded again. "Yes, that's a yes."

Belle stopped dead in her tracks and stared at Cade, who stared right back at her. "And you don't mind if I come along, too?" she asked.

"I don't mind," Michael said, quite seriously.

"But if you're afraid of tarantulas, recluse spiders, black widows, and scorpions, you'll have to sleep in the car."

Cade paused for a moment, the look on his face completely unreadable, then suddenly he burst out laughing. "She's afraid of common houseflies, too," he said.

"I know," Michael replied. "And grasshoppers, and bees, and moths."

"I am not afraid of moths!" Belle chimed in.

"Then why do you always scream when you see one?" Michael countered, chancing a quick, mischievous look at her to gauge her reaction.

"I don't scream. I just—well, sometimes I gasp if I'm startled."

"Scream," he contradicted. "Not gasp. And if we build a fire when we're camping, it will attract moths. Then you'll scream."

Michael was teasing Belle. Cade saw it, and was surprised as it was a side of his son he hadn't known existed. And the whole bug thing…that nearly brought a lump to his throat, thinking back to those summer days with his little brother. Days he wished to God he could get back and do better. "I'd like to build a fire, and cook our dinner over it. And, Belle…" He looked directly at her, and winked. "You're welcome to sit with Michael and me near the fire, but you've got to control yourself."

"Control myself?" she asked, playing along.

"Control yourself, Mom," Michael answered in place of Cade. "Moths won't hurt you. Although studies show that they're not bothered by high-pitched sounds, so if you have to scream, it won't hurt their hearing."

"How do you know that, Michael?" she asked, utterly surprised.

He shrugged, completely indifferent to her reaction. "I read it somewhere."

She looked at Cade again. "And it stayed with him."

"Because I like bugs, Mom. You know that!"

Another lump came to Cade's throat, caused by even more painful memories from some other time. "Do you know what entomology is?" Cade asked, struggling to recover.

Michael looked perplexed for a moment, then shook his head.

"Entomology is the study of insects. An entomologist is a specialist who makes his or her career out of studying insects." His son liked bugs and that made him pretty typical of most boys his age. It also made him so much like Robbie, Cade didn't know how to deal with it. "What's your favorite insect?" he asked, his voice shaky.

Michael scrunched his face into a frown for a second, thinking. Then his eyes lit up, and he smiled. "Moths!"

"I think your two are ganging up on me," Belle said, her attention totally focused on Cade.

"Maybe because you deserve it, Belle," Cade responded. He'd caught her stare, saw the question in her eyes. Felt the guilt over it. But what was done was done. Leaving Belle out of something important in his life all those years ago was something else he couldn't take back or undo.

"Yeah," Michael echoed. "Because you deserve it."

And just like that Cade's bond with Michael started to form. All these years, and all it took was a moth. It choked him up, actually. So much so he had to turn away to blink back the tears for Michael, tears for Robbie. Tears for himself and what he'd lost.

* * *

She hadn't seen much of Texas, yet. There weren't enough hours in her day to do everything she wanted. Hardly enough to do what she had to do, and if she had extra time, sightseeing certainly was not at the top of Belle's list of priorities. But this was a pleasant place to camp, she did have to admit, and, thankfully, close enough for her connectivity, so she didn't feel completely guilty, or nervous.

Cade had chosen a little patch of land on the back half of a ranch that surely looked desolate, compared to the front half, something totally removed from the structure of civilization, but not so much that she felt isolated and not at all what she'd expected. Barren was what came to mind first, when she thought about Texas in general. Wide open spaces, naked land, nothing green unless she carted along a tossed salad. Yet this—it was breathtaking. A lush, rocky little area, with lots of trees and grass, and a pristine stream running through the middle of it. And the sky...oh, my gosh, the sky. It was an eternal azure blue, so pretty all she wanted to do was lie down and look up at it, for hours, or days.

No, this was definitely not the Texas she'd

thought she'd be getting on this little outing. In fact, this place Cade had picked out was so nice, she daydreamed of a house here. Maybe a sprawling ranch-style up on the rise overlooking this perfect little valley. Something high enough to get the full view of the area yet secluded enough so as not to be seen from any of the dirt roads or vantage points nearby.

For now, that was all wishful thinking. She was barely scraping by, paying rent on the two-bedroom Southwestern bungalow sitting adjacent to her office, running her medical practice, squirreling away every spare penny to buy it. Still, she could hope for more. Hope for her ranch-style home on a scenic bluff someday. Somewhere sumptuous, like this. "Guess I didn't expect anything so beautiful," she said, dropping her just-bought pup tent on the ground, then falling to her knees next to it. "Except for a couple of the major cities, and Big Badger, I haven't really seen much of Texas."

"It's a beautiful state, Belle. People get the wrong impression all the time, but we have scenery here that's as pretty as anything you'll find anywhere else in the world."

She smiled, tickled by his response to her naivety. More than that, amazed by the feelings of home that still ran deep in him. She'd never seen that side of him before. "Watch it, Cade. You're beginning to sound like you could live here again. You know, big-city doctor returns to his country roots." She wasn't sure Cade could actually do that, though. He loved his conveniences and out here they were few and far between. "Not that you'd ever do that, would you?" she asked.

But he didn't answer. Instead, he simply stared off into the wide open spaces. Stared so long it made her uncomfortable. "You wouldn't actu-ally—" she began, but he cut her off.

"You never know," he said.

Cade, back in Texas? That was something she wouldn't have anticipated. "You're not thinking about it, are you?"

He turned to face her. "What I'm thinking about are the pup tents, and getting them pitched before dark."

Something was definitely going on with him. Something she didn't know, or understand. Was it the real reason for his spur-of-the-moment de-cision to take a leave of absence from his practice and come here? The real reason for some of the changes, or differences, she was seeing in him? "Starting a fire would be good, too, since I'd like to fix something to eat before it gets dark."

"Can I cook the hot dogs?" Michael asked, suddenly animated, as the cricket he'd been stalking was totally forgotten. "All by myself?"

Cade deferred to Belle for that answer by tipping his hat and nodding at her.

She answered, "Before we can cook hot dogs, we need to set up a camp, then go find the right kind of sticks to put the hot dogs on. Which chore do you want, Michael?"

"Sticks."

"Long ones," she said. "Not too big around, since the hot dog has got to slip down over the end of it. How about you find them, and your dad can come cut them?"

"No knife?" Michael asked. "I wanted to cut the sticks."

Belle shook her head. Saw the sullenness creeping into her son already. His intelligence might be way above the norm, but there was always the fine line of his age, and seven was too young to do half the things he wanted to do, and knew he could do. "No knife, just like at home. But maybe if your dad goes with you, he can show you how to cut the sticks with a pocket knife, so you'll know for when you're older."

"Or clippers," Cade said, pulling a hand-held pair from his hip pocket then handing them to Michael. "Safety catch, easy to use, great for hot dog sticks." He grinned. "Belle, while you put up both tents—"

"Both tents?"

"Can't help it. Michael and I have other chores to do." He glanced at his son, who was back on his hands and knees again, looking at another bug.

"Then I'll put up the tents. But I think you're on the stick detail by yourself."

"You never insist on anything when he gets distracted like that, do you?" Cade asked, fighting to keep in the annoyance that had suddenly flared. But it wasn't about Michael, or even Belle. It was about himself, and so many lost opportunities. Sure, there were any number of things he could teach his son, but would he be here when Michael got to put that learning to practical use? Would he be here to experience the pride that came of his son's accomplishments? "You just—" There was no point finishing the sentence because he wasn't going to drag his son into this. Instead, he slapped both his hands against his thighs, and spun to walk way.

But Belle grabbed him by the arm and held on. "Look, I don't know what this is about, and it's obvious you don't think it's any of my business. But in case it's me, or leftover feelings about us, I just want you to know that no matter what's happened between us, I've gotten through most of the hard feelings and I'm really not against you the way I used to be." She let go of his arm. "And if it's about Michael, he doesn't mean to shut you out, Cade. That's just the way he is sometimes. Nothing personal."

"I appreciate that. And what I said about never insisting—"

"With Michael, you learn to pick your battles. In the whole scheme of things, that wasn't one of them."

"But what is, Belle?" he asked, stopping but not turning round to face her. "And how do we decide what's worth it, and what's not? Because I don't know."

She glanced down at Michael, who was making friends with some black, multi-legged thing sprinting through the dirt. "Sometimes it's a guess, sometimes intuition. And as often as not it's just about the mood I'm in."

He chuckled. "What? Is that Belle Carter confessing she doesn't have all the answers?"

She leaned in closer to him, then whispered, "That's Belle Carter confessing that most of the time she doesn't have any of the answers, she just fakes it." She straightened back up. "And if you repeat that to anybody, especially to Maudie, I'll cut your cowboy hat to shreds."

"Not my hat!" he exclaimed.

In one quick motion, Belle snatched the hat off Cade's head, then put it on and patted it into place. "And what I said about not being against you—I meant it, Cade. I'm not." With that, she turned and sashayed away.

And, oh, what a sashay it was. One the likes of which he'd never seen on any woman, lady doc or cowboy, anywhere before. And one he wasn't likely to forget any time soon.

"He's exhausted," Belle said, settling down across the campfire from Cade. "Went to sleep the instant he crawled into the sleeping bag." Much to her surprise. Normally, Michael was a bit of a problem at bedtime. He always had more things he wanted to do, play one more set in a game, read one more chapter in a book, watch one more television show. An active mind never ready to settle down. But tonight she was pleased. Camping agreed with him. And so far it hadn't been so bad on her either.

"You enjoying yourself?" Cade asked.

"I think I am. It's nice being away from responsibility, even if it's only for a few minutes. It's been a long time since I could just step out of myself for a little while. Even now, having you here, sharing responsibility for Michael, it means a lot to me."

"I feel guilty as hell because I can't do more to help you. And guilty as hell because I never seem to succeed with Michael the way I want to, no matter how hard I try."

"You don't need to feel guilty about me. I'm good on my own. As for Michael, maybe you should try not trying so hard. You know, let up a little. Quit forcing yourself to succeed the way you want to and try succeeding with Michael the way he wants it. Because Michael does have opinions and likes and dislikes, just like the rest of us do. But he responds differently, so sometimes you're better off letting him adjust however he wants to rather than imposing your own parameters on that adjustment."

"I do that?"

"Yep. You did it with me when we were married, always trying to make me fit into your box, your set of definitions and boundaries. So you do it without thinking. Besides that, it's part of trying to be a good parent, I think. You know, wanting your child to try to fit inside your own boundaries, hoping he'll turn out to be a smaller version of you. And I'm as guilty of that as you are. The thing is, I know I have to make allowances for Michael's Asperger's, and there are times it's tough because for me the conflict—my own personal conflict—is always about letting him find his own way or me finding it for him. As his mom, I want to find it for him, to make his life easier. But that's my need coming out, not his."

"And my need is to find any way to parent him."

"From your heart, Cade. That's where you start. Instead of beating yourself up because you don't think you do it good enough, maybe stop trying to make all the little details fit into a nice, tidy little puzzle and accept the fact that sometimes the pieces fit together even if they're not quite in the right place. It may distort the picture you're trying to create, or it may make it more interesting, depending on the way you look at the world." She gazed up at the black sky, and sighed. "Anyway, if it's of any consolation, I'm glad I came out here with you two, even with the bugs. But I think I'm going to head back to town early tomorrow, probably before Michael gets up in the morning. If you don't mind."

"Not on my account, I hope."

"Actually, on my account. Like I said, I don't get a lot of time for myself, and barring medical emergencies it would be nice to have a few hours just to..." She smiled. "Soak in the tub. Maybe get my hair cut. Buy a new pair of shoes and not have to worry about Michael, because I know he's safe with his dad."

"I've missed you, Belle."

She picked up a stick and poked at the fire, sending wisps of smoke and red-lit ash up into the night-time sky. "I know how that feels," she said. "I spent too much of my time missing you, but maybe that's the way it was meant to be. I think we started at the wrong place, Cade." She looked across at him, remembering all the reasons she'd loved him. And there were more than there were reasons not to love him. But the reasons not to love him had been so overwhelming. "I don't regret it, though. I think you and me, as a couple, through the good and bad of it, gave me a different balance than I would have had if we hadn't been together."

"A good balance?"

"The best." She tossed the stick aside, and stood up. "Being divorced isn't bad. I love my life the way it is now. Wouldn't trade it for anything. When we were married, I wasn't...happy. Not the way I wanted to be, or expected that I could be. Part of that was you, part of that was me. Probably because we were suited in some ways yet in so many ways we weren't, and those were the ways that mattered most. Then when Michael came along, and after he was diagnosed, I had choices to make, lots of them. I was finishing medical school, trying to decide what kind of medical practice I wanted, coming to grips with what I'd have to do for Michael. It was tough on me, and you weren't there for a lot of it. In the end, though, the only real choice I knew I had to make was to find a life that made me happy, because I couldn't be the kind of mother Michael needed if I wasn't."

"And you're happy without me. You don't even know how lousy that makes me feel when I hear you say something like that."

She smiled. "But I am happy. Happier than I've ever been. Not because we're not together any more, but because of me. All I ever wanted, Cade, was a home, a child, a good medical practice. I told you that when we got married, and kept telling you, over and over. But you never seemed to hear it. Then when you accepted that surgical post in Thailand without even discussing it with me, then the one after that in Chicago— Anyway, I've got everything I want now, and I doubt there are very many people who can make the same claim."

"It was six months. Thailand was six months, then I was coming back."

"And I'm glad it worked out for you. So please be glad this is working out for me, because this is where we're settling, just the two of us."

"Then marriage doesn't figure into that happiness equation somewhere in your future?"

"Once burned—and the thing is, marriage isn't the cure-all for everything that ails you. What I've discovered is that I do life pretty good without it. So why rock that proverbial boat?"

"Maybe because if you rock the boat often enough, some time there might be a ripple effect that will rock your world. And you deserve that, Belle."

"You rocked my world once, Cade. Then turned it into an earthquake. This time around, I like the ground a little more solid underneath my feet. But you know what? I've missed you, too." Tall, handsome, maybe even better than he'd been when they'd met, she wondered if any other man could ever affect her the way Cade had then, and even now. A long time ago she'd decided no one could, and lived with that. Taking a step closer, she stood on tiptoe and brushed a tender kiss to his lips. "I've definitely missed you. Anyway, it's time to turn in, and hope there aren't any little creatures crawling into my sleeping bag."

"Goodnight, Belle," he said, raising his hands to his lips as he watched her walk to her tent.

Inside the tent, Michael let the door flap drop back into place then made a fast lunge for his sleeping bag. He'd barely wiggled in when Belle crawled into the tent and stretched out on her bag. Even though she looked over at him, in the dark she didn't see the grin that had spread ear to ear the moment he'd seen his mom kiss his dad. A grin that hadn't faded the least little bit as he lay there in the dark, thinking about it. She also didn't see the little hand tucked down beside him in his sleeping bag, the one with crossed fingers.

Like he'd needed that kiss! Sleep had been elusive lately anyway, and now there was no way it was going to happen tonight. Not for quite a while anyway. Because Belle had kissed him. "Damn," he muttered, kicking dirt into the fire. It didn't mean anything. He knew that. Didn't delude himself into thinking there was any significance in it whatsoever. Still, one little kiss and he was a mess.

Rather than hanging around the campsite and risking doing something that would disturb Belle or Michael, Cade wandered down the path to the creek, well within sight of the camp. He sat down on the bank and, with the light of the moon casting a perfect silvery beam down on him, watched the water churn over the rock bed. The water itself was pure, a vital source of life. And the rock bed impeded its progress. Yet the water got through it anyway. Found its path along its course without much struggle. In some ways, his life was that rock bed, he thought. An impediment to good, a hindrance to a vital life source. One way or another, that's what he'd been doing for the better part of his life—living outside his life, not fitting in. Impeding the progress. First, there had been Robbie. Then Belle, and even Michael.

Sure, maybe there was a little bit of self-pity mixed into his emotions, but mostly he was just… frustrated. And tired of the struggle. Not sure if he could move from the outside back in, though. So that's why the nights turned into his enemy so often. They were filled with the memories he couldn't put away. Filled with the struggles that got put aside for other things during the day, but always seemed to find their way back after dark.

"I have nights like this every now and then," Belle said, sitting down on the creek bank next to him. "You can't sleep and the night seems eternally long. So you pace or read a book or listen to music, hoping something will do the trick. Yet an hour later, two hours later, three hours later nothing has changed, and you're alone with your thoughts, and the things that frustrate and scare you."

"The things you can't change in your life," he said, scooting over a little to accommodate her.

"Some things you can't change. And some things probably shouldn't be changed. Most things I think you can, though, if you want the changes bad enough."

"Like the divorce. I didn't want it, Belle. Fought like hell to hang on."

"But too late. Because that was the change I wanted. The thing you couldn't change and the thing I wanted badly enough to change. It's what we had to do, Cade."

"That's what I keep telling myself on nights like this. The thing is, I wasn't cut out for marriage, but I sure as hell wasn't cut out for divorce either."

Belle laughed. "Then I'd say you're caught in quite the conundrum."

"How did you know I was out here?"

"I didn't. But after I lay down, I discovered

I wasn't in the mood to sleep either. So I came down here because it's so...peaceful." She pulled her feet up and unlaced her shoes. "Care to go wading with me?" she asked, glancing back at the campsite to make sure Michael wasn't stirring the way his parents were.

"There could be bugs in that water. Since the only light we've got is the moon, you might not be able to see them."

"I'll take my chances," she said slipping her feet into the water. Then sighing. "Haven't done this since I was a child. Used to be afraid to do it, actually. We had this little creek that ran out behind our house, and it was full of these little crawdads, as we called them. Technically, I think they're called crayfish. Anyway, they have claws, and I was scared to death of getting my toes pinched. Thing was, it really didn't even hurt when they got you. But I missed out on some good wading because of my fears." She kicked a little water, then bent down and scooped some into her hands and splashed it at Cade. "Coming in?"

"Oh, yeah," he said, his voice suddenly full of the devil. "And you'd better watch out because there are much more dangerous things in this

creek other than the crawdads." He pulled off
his boots, tossed aside his hat, and jumped into
the water with full force, and the first thing he
did was splash Belle back. "You know, I'm good
at this. We had a little creek behind our house,
too, and…" But by the time Robbie had been old
enough to enjoy playing in that creek, Cade had
already moved on to other things. Try as he might,
he couldn't recall a time when he'd waded with
Robbie or even splashed around with him.

"Cade? Where are you? You wandered off."

He shook his head to shake off the melancho-
lia. "I'm right here, getting ready to soak you," he
said, then grabbed hold of Belle's hand and pulled
her over to him.

She fought to get free, but not too much. "What
are you going to do?" she asked cautiously.

"What makes you think I'm going to do anything?" He held on a little tighter, not enough
to hurt but enough to ensure she wasn't getting
away without a struggle. Playing just like a kid
would, he thought. And all his broodings seemed
to magically splash away, too. Because of Belle?
he wondered.

"I think the question should be, what would

make me think you're not going to do something, Cade Carter? Because you know you will."

He thought about it, but only for a second, then without the slightest bit of warning let go of her hand, wrapped both his arms around Belle, pulled her tight to his chest, then dunked them both into the water. It wasn't deep, didn't cover them, and it wasn't cold. But the shock of it caused her to gasp. When she did, he let go of her, and that's when the battle began. She splashed him, he splashed her. And laughed… Cade couldn't remember laughing so much since, well, he couldn't remember when. "This is crazy," he sputtered, making a lunge for her hand to pull her under again.

She escaped him, and had enough time to reverse his plan by grabbing hold of his hand and pulling him under the water. But her reverse was met by his, and the next thing she knew, she was sprawled on top of Cade in six inches of water, precariously close to him. Awkwardly close to him. He saw it in her face, saw the change from happy and playful to—it wasn't fear. Maybe surprise? Or trepidation?

Whatever it was, it caused her to push off him, and didn't allow him to stop her. But he stayed there in the water as she scrambled for the bank. He fully expected her to pick up her shoes and run straight back to her tent. But she didn't. She simply stood there and looked at him for a moment. "What?" he finally asked, standing up now that the moment was truly over.

"Just thinking about the good times."

"Does that come with an asterisk? One that indicates, at the bottom of the page, that thinking about the bad times comes next?"

"Not really. Sometimes it's nice to remember only the things we did the right way and pretend the rest of it never happened. Anyway, I'll wake you up in the morning so you can look after Michael when I leave. And, Cade…thank you."

It might have been the moment they would have kissed had they been lovers. He wasn't even sure that Belle would reject him if he tried. Right now, though, he liked the friendship. Maybe that's what they'd missed the first time—the friendship. Anyway, he had an idea that friendship would be the nice, soft pillow he needed to help him sleep tonight. So he waded out of the creek, put on his boots, picked up his hat, and carried his soggy self back to his tent. For the first time in years, sleeping alone wasn't going to feel quite so...alone.

Seeing his parents heading back up the trail, one by one, Michael scurried up the trail to get to the tent before his mother did. When she finally entered, he was fully involved in the best fake sleep of his life. Fingers on both hands crossed this time.

"Interested in trying something new?" Cade asked. The morning had been rough. Belle left early, as she'd said she would, and Michael was in a bad mood. He wasn't saying why, but Cade could only guess that he'd expected his mother there, not his father, when he woke up. For that, he couldn't blame the kid. Sometimes life's surprises weren't the easiest to deal with.

"I want to go home now," Michael said, in his best matter-of-fact voice. "Right now, please. I want to go home."

Like he hadn't heard that a hundred times this past half-hour. "There's something I want to show you, first."

Michael shook his head vehemently. "It's time to go home."

How did you fight against that? Belle probably knew, and since his connectivity out here was as good as hers, he thought about calling her. Pulled his cellphone from his pocket, started to dial. Then what? he asked himself. Admit defeat? Tell her she'd been right all along, that this camping trip was a bad idea, and not realizing that made him a bad father? Hell, no, he wouldn't admit it. Wouldn't admit anything to her. "We will. But we're going on a hike first," he said, stuffing his phone back in his pocket. "Maybe we'll find some interesting bugs."

"I wouldn't mind looking for a whirligig beetle." Michael's eyes lit up with sudden interest. "They live in the plants along the water, and like to go swimming."

"Then maybe we can find one in the stream." And start the second phase of this camping trip.

"Can we go now?" Michael asked anxiously. "Before breakfast?"

Now he was willing to stay through breakfast? Sure, it was a little step, but little steps led to bigger ones. "Sounds like the best time to me. Oh, and grab that black bag sitting over there next to my backpack. There's something in it I want to show you."

"A present?" he asked, his interest definitely piqued.

"Yes, if you like it."

"A video game?"

Cade shook his head. "Better than a video game."

"I don't think so," Michael replied, hefting the bag then simply holding it, looking at it from all angles. Studying its contours, its fabric, its strap. "Unless it's two video games."

"Take a look inside," Cade said, then literally caught himself holding his breath. He wanted this to work so badly.

Slowly, with the patience of a saint, Michael unzipped the bag, inch by everlasting inch, studying the zipper teeth as they parted, occasionally re-zipping part of the bag then taking the same course again. Only after nearly a minute of zipping and unzipping, when he reached the end of that journey, did he finally look inside. "It's a camera!" Michael said, grabbing it out and looking almost excited about it. "Is for me?" he asked.

"Sure is. I thought you might like to take photos

of the things that interest you—bugs, for example. That whirling beetle, if we find one."

"Whirligig," Michael corrected as he studied the camera for a moment, clicked the button that extended the lens, then held the camera up to his eye to look through the viewfinder.

"OK, whirligig. So how about we go down to the creek and see what we can find?"

Michael looked at his dad through the camera, saw him come into focus, saw the way his dad looked at him, not smiling. Maybe his dad was sad, the way his mother was sometimes. Last night, though, they'd looked happy, playing in the creek. Too bad he hadn't had the camera then.

"Ready, Dad," Michael said, then snapped a photo. "Now let's go find some bugs."

CHAPTER FIVE

"IT'S a bee sting," Belle said, looking at the red welts on Cade's arm. "Actually, about a dozen of them. What happened?"

"A hornet, not a bee," he said defensively. "And there are thirteen, to be exact."

"I'm afraid to ask," she said, pulling a tube of topical corticosteroid from her supply closet then turning back to face him, "but how?"

"There was a hornets' nest in the garage eaves at the boarding house, and—"

"Let me guess. You were being your ever-charming self, trying to appeal to the admiring masses by volunteering to get rid of it." Applying a measure of the ointment to a swab, she dabbed it to the first welt on Cade's forearm. "Did you even check to see if it was an active hornets' nest?"

"You always do that, don't you, Belle? Even after all this time, you still jump to conclusions—

the worst conclusions when it comes to something, anything, about me."

"Well, I think I have reason." Raising her eyes to meet his, she cut him with her glance. A look meant to challenge. Or wound. "Because you always left Michael and me when a good cause came your way. What else am I supposed to think?"

"I wasn't ready to settle down, Belle. No excuses. I was a bad husband. All that responsibility scared me. I admitted it to you then, and I'll admit it to you now. Married life wasn't—wasn't what I'd expected it to be. And I struggled."

"You struggled, and I jumped to the conclusion that you were a bad husband when—let's see. Was it the first, second, or maybe the third time you went your merry way in the world without even mentioning it to me? Remember that, Cade? I'd wake up in the morning, find a note on your pillow saying you've gone to Cambodia or Haiti. Good humanitarian causes, but you never checked to see what kind of humanitarian needs your wife and son had. So I guess jumping to the worst conclusion about you has become a Pavlovian response because you conditioned it in me." She returned her attention to treating his welts. "I'm sorry, Cade. I don't want to be bitter about this any more, but sometimes it pops out."

He chuckled. "You still hold your own with the best of them, Belladonna. That's one of the things I always admired most about you. You're a force."

"Who doesn't always want to be reckoned with," she added. "And for me to jump to the conclusion that you tried to help someone isn't assuming the worst. That's who you are, and sometimes I think I'm a little envious of it. You never asked me to go, Cade. Not once. And I might have, before Michael came along, to do the same work that caught you up, get to know you that way, and maybe even to see what it was that took you away from me. But you always left, half the time never bothering to tell me, and you can't even begin to know how that feels, always getting left behind."

"Because I was stupid, immature…" he said, gritting his teeth against the sting. "I'm sorry we didn't talk more while we were married, because I didn't know you would have gone."

"To save my marriage, I would have gone. And I think we talked. We simply didn't say the right words at the right times. Anyway, your stings—

how did the hornets beat you? That's not me judging you now, Cade. I want to know."

"You want to know because you think it's going to be embarrassing."

They made eye contact once more, only this time there was laughter in her eyes. "Maybe you deserve some embarrassment."

"Well, sorry to disappoint you, but Mr. Parker was up on the ladder, teetering. He's too old be climbing around like that, so I—"

"You traded places." Said with modest appreciation. "Which is a good thing, Cade."

"Good or not, let me tell you, for someone in his upper seventies, he runs like a man half his age. When I knocked that nest down, and at least a million angry hornets came screaming out of it—"

"Wouldn't there have been an easier way?" Spraying them would have been easier, but that's something Cade would never do...never intentionally kill any creature. Not even one with a stinger meant for him. His gentleness was one of the first things she'd adored about him.

"Maybe. But my idea was to dislodge their nest, agitate them, and hope they'd scatter. Which they did, actually." He paused. Cringed. "Straight into the house."

"What?"

"Open kitchen window."

"By way of your arm first." Thirteen stings had to hurt and Cade was lucky he wasn't allergic, or this could have turned serious. Still, the mental image of Cade versus the hornets—there was a time she would have wished this on him. Not any more. Truth was, she liked him better in divorce than she had in marriage. He'd matured, and mellowed. It fit him well.

"Better me than Mr. Parker, I guess," he said, wincing each time she dabbed a different welt. "Although I've got to tell you, Mrs. Parker was angrier than the hornets at both her husband and me."

"Did you get all the hornets out of her house?"

"Hornets seem to beget hornets, I think. They're everywhere. So the Parkers have gone to Dallas to stay with their daughter for a couple of days, while someone here tries to smoke them out of the house. Apparently, the better way to go about this whole thing would have been to wait until night, when they're dormant, close all the house windows, then build a fire underneath the nest. They don't like smoke, so they would have left without much drama. Something about beating the nest with a stick didn't put them in a very good mood, I suppose." He tried grinning, but winced instead.

"But no one else got stung, did they?"

"Nope. Just me."

Belle cringed. "I'm sorry, Cade. I'm sorry about doubting you, sorry I automatically thought the worst, and I'm sorry this happened. You were trying to do a good deed, and—"

"And you haven't seen the ones on my back yet. They got me through my shirt, Belle. Those little beggars ganged up on me. Had a huge grudge to carry out."

"There's more?"

"Don't know how many. But my back's on fire. Hurts worse than my arm, which hurts pretty damned bad."

"Then take your shirt off," she said, returning to the supply cabinet for more swabs. "And just in case, I think I'm going to give you a shot of antihistamine."

"Or whiskey," he muttered, beginning to unbutton his blue chambray shirt ever so gingerly.

"Since when did you start drinking?" He had his share of faults, but the common vices weren't included in those. Cade took care of his body, something she'd appreciated when they were married, something she was afraid she was still going to appreciate once she turned around.

"Since right about now—the same time you're probably going to want to start drinking."

She turned to face him, kept her eyes purposely fixed on his. "What's that supposed to mean?"

"Since the boarding house is temporarily closed down, you know that spare room above your garage?"

"No." She shook her head. Thought about it. Shook her head again. "No way. You can't possibly think you're going to..."

"But you're not using it, are you? And wasn't it an efficiency apartment at one time? So it's got a bathroom. All I need is a bed, or a cot, and I'll be fine. It'll be good for Michael, too."

"Good for Michael? How do you figure?"

"I'll be closer to him, so we'll have more time—"

She thrust out her hand to stop him. "This isn't about Michael. It's about me. And I don't want to

live with you, Cade. Did it once, remember? And
it didn't work out well."

"Me staying in the room over your detached
garage, which is all the way to the back of your
property, a whole yard away from your house,
is hardly living together. Besides, if you don't
take me in, I'm going to have to go to Newman
for a room, and that's a twenty-minute drive one
way. Everything here in Big Badger, which is ten
rooms at the Fourth Street Motel, is booked for the
next few days. Of course, when my back isn't so
sore, I can go and camp at the Ruda del Monte."

"Spare me," she said, slapping the swab pack-
ets down on the exam table. "You can stay, but
that doesn't give you house privileges. I'm serious about that. You can't just come and go in my
life as you please. And that includes my house,
even if you are living in my garage—wounded."

He dropped his shirt on the exam table. "Fine.
I'll respect that. Oh, and that antihistamine shot?
I'm going to pass. I want to see a few patients before I go home today, and the antihistamine will
make me groggy."

"You don't have to do that. I can see them for
you."

"I know you can, but so can I." He grinned, then groaned when she treated a particularly angry welt. "Besides, if I don't keep myself busy, all I'm going to do is sit around and grumble about feeling miserable."

"Well, the offer will stay open if you start feeling worse. Same goes for an antihistamine. You know where the syringes are, and how much to take if you change your mind. And, Cade, really. You don't have to push yourself. You're not having an allergic reaction to the stings, which is good, but you've got so many of them—"

"I appreciate the concern, Belle. I know you assumed, well—when you said I was trying to ingratiate myself with the masses was a little harsh, but sometimes that's been the easiest thing for me to do, rather than face up to what I needed to."

"And all the time we were together, you never told me why. Maybe that's the saddest thing of all, Cade. We were married, yet we weren't." Belle actually gasped when she saw the mess his back was in. Seventeen welts in all, when she counted. "OK, I understand why you don't want the antihistamine right now, but do you want something for pain? A small dose with codeine take the edge off?" she asked.

"Oh, so you're feeling sorry for me now?" he asked, fighting back a gasp of his own as her fingers skimmed lightly over each sting.

Yes, she was. She was definitely feeling sorry for him trying to make himself comfortable on that cot in the garage apartment. Suddenly, an image of Cade sprawled across her bed flashed before her eyes and she tried hard to blink it away before it took hold. "How about I offer you one night, two at the most, in a real bed? It'll be more comfortable for you than a cot."

"I wasn't complaining about the garage."

"Maybe not, but you haven't seen your back, and no way that cot's going to work. So you can have my bed, and I'll take—"

"The left side, if you want it. I won't cross the line, promise."

"I sleep on the right side now. And I don't care if you cross the line because I'll be downstairs, on the couch." Safe. OK, so maybe the offer was tempting. She'd always liked waking up next to him, feeling so safe, so connected, even when their connection had been starting to break. But now? Cade wasn't serious about the offer. Or did he think they could simply crawl into bed together to find some of what they'd lost? Whichever, the mere suggestion of something that wasn't them any more tweaked her nerves as it made her think about things that could never happen, and things she didn't want to know she still wished for. "You should have stayed in Chicago, Cade," she snapped. "You could have stuck to the original plan, stayed at your job, spent six weeks with Michael at the end of summer like we'd agreed on, and none of this would have happened."

"I was stung by some hornets. It's not the end of the world, Belle."

Maybe not the end of the world, but it was beginning to feel like she was being stung. And just when she'd thought she was impervious.

"I'm concerned about the growing number of *E. coli* cases," Belle said, dropping down into the chair next to Cade, who was busy jotting notes into a patient chart. He was sitting on a wooden stool, not looking any too comfortable about it. But at least his back wasn't touching anything. Neither was his arm. It was a small lounge, though, the best she could do considering space constraints. She'd turned one of the supply closets into a staff lounge and crammed in one small love seat, a table with a coffee-maker, microwave oven, and a mini-fridge. Inventive use of minimal space. Or, at least, that's what she'd thought until she had to sit knee to knee with Cade. And touching knees, even through his denim and her linen, gave her a little jolt. "Another of the ranches called in with a couple of sick ranch hands. Maybe a couple more, the manager wasn't sure. Ranch owner and his family are fine so far, though. So I'm going out to have a look in about an hour."

"But you've sent everything you can find to the lab and no results?"

"No results. And, actually, I'm using two different labs to make sure I'm getting consistent results. The thing is, Cade, I have enough cases now to call it an outbreak, which I don't want to do because that will cause a panic. I'm new here, people don't trust me yet, especially the men, and if I get more aggressive, make that official call to the state health department for help, you know how the scenario will play itself out. Alerting the public to be cautious, I'm the hero if it is a real outbreak and the villain if it's not. There's no gray area in that, and since I haven't found a source yet, it's not responsible to sound the alarm when I can't even tell them if they should avoid bean sprouts, lettuce, well water, or dirt in general."

"Well, you're right about that. It's better to err on the side of caution rather than cause a mass panic. But that's only going to go on for so long, then you'll be called irresponsible no matter which way it turns out." He shut his chart, set it aside, and twisted to face her. "I think it's cattle related, Belle. We're in the heart of cattle country, all the ranches around here raise cattle, and half the town residents are involved in the industry somehow."

"But I've had the local beef tested, several times, and...nothing."

"The thing is, without taking mass cultures of everything, and I mean everything around here—"

"We're stuck. More people get sick and I'm in deep trouble. Damned if you do, damned if you don't. But you've seen what happens when health warnings go out. You link the bacterium that's making everybody sick to the cattle, and the people will—well, I don't want to think about what they'll do. It could decimate the town's economy, though. People in panic mode, normal, rational people otherwise, will go to extremes, and I don't want to be responsible for that. The problem is, since I've been sending samples to the county lab, as well as a private one, I'm not sure how much longer I can keep this quiet. The county health officials are on my side about discretion so far, and they've even had a couple of investigators kicking around to see what they can find. But at some point word's going to leak out no matter what happens. I mean, right now people think it's only a stomach bug going round, which is really what it is. But attach the word outbreak or endemic to it, which will happen when we go public, and we're in big trouble." She sighed heavily. "Either way, time's running out."

"For what it's worth, I think you're doing the right thing. It's a tough choice, Belle. I think the people here are luckier to have you than they know."

"Yeah, well, tell that to the lynch mob when they come to get me." She stood, then walked around Cade, stopping at the back of his chair.

Gently, she lifted his shirt to have a look at his back. "Can I give you something yet?"

"Sympathy?"

She smiled. There were so many things about Cade that hadn't worked for her when they were married. Yet there were so many things that had worked, and still did. Overall, she was glad he was here, for Michael's sake. Maybe even a little for hers. "Goodnight, Cade. Will you lock up when you leave?"

"He might be hungry," Michael said, aiming his camera directly at his mother while she dumped the spaghetti into to colander to drain it.

Belle was glad he was taking such interest in his photography, but he must have snapped fifty shots of her fixing dinner, and fifty before that, when she was stretched out on the couch, barefooted, hair a mess, reading a medical article. "There are plenty of places in town where your father can get something to eat," she said, turning her back to Michael before he snapped another picture of her, one where she looked annoyed. Because she was annoyed. All these years later, and she was still letting Cade get to her. Too many thoughts about him, too many memories. "And I think he's pretty tired. I'm sure he's asleep by now."

"But his light's on," Michael argued.

Of course Cade's light was on, and here was her son wanting his dad to come for dinner. How could she refuse that? The answer was, she couldn't. "OK, go knock on his door. Tell him dinner will be ready in ten minutes, if he'd like to join us. Then come and help me set the table."

Without a word, Michael ran out the door and straight to the garage, pausing only a fraction of a second at the steps before bolting up them. He was so agile, so athletic, it made her proud. Especially when she thought back to the day when the specialist had told her what to anticipate from a child diagnosed with Asperger's syndrome. Certainly, physical ability hadn't been on the list of expectations. Rather, she'd been told to look for clumsiness. And look at him, a true seven-year-old athlete who didn't know what he was supposed to lack, or not achieve in life.

She watched as Michael banged on the door the first time, waited a moment, then knocked again. No answer. So he tried a third time, and by his fourth attempt Belle was out in the yard, on her way to the garage. "Michael," she yelled. "Maybe he's not home."

"But I heard his music."

Classical. Mozart. She hated Mozart. He'd always thought she loved it, insisted that she did. But she preferred something more meaty, like Beethoven. Another one of their differences, as it turned out. And, Mozart was definitely blaring away in the apartment, which, for some unperceived reason, alerted her. Cold chills shot up her arms, and she immediately bolted into her house to grab her medical bag then ran right back into the yard. "Michael, would you go back into the house and make sure the front door is shut and locked?" She wasn't sure what she'd find once she got into the apartment, but she was sure she didn't want Michael finding it with her. "Then set the table for dinner, please." Hopefully, this was her being an alarmist, and Cade was off somewhere, having dinner. She was trying to think positively even though a second round of cold chills assaulted her.

"Can I see Dad, first?" he asked, turning to jiggle the doorknob.

"It's locked, sweetheart, so please don't try to

open it." Belle jumped between Michael and the door, then pointed to the house. "Check the front door," she reminded him, then waited until he'd scampered away before she tried the apartment door, found it locked, then pulled out her master key and stuck it in the lock.

"Cade," she gasped when she was inside, and discovered his lifeless form on the floor next to the cot. She ran over to him and dropped to her knees. First instinct, find a pulse. It was there. Weak, thready, but beating away, thank God. Second thing, she put her ear to his chest to listen for breath sounds, heard clear gurgling and wheezing. "What did you do, Cade?" she choked, shoving back the coffee table to give her more room to assess his pupillary action. Good. Equal, reactive. No head trauma that she could discern. And a quick check from his neck down revealed no other kind of trauma.

She actually paused, like she expected a response from him. But that lasted only a second before she was back, examining, listening, observing. Looking for anything.

"It was locked," Michael said from the doorway. "What's wrong with him?"

It was too late to hide anything now. "He wasn't feeling well earlier today, and I haven't checked him enough to see what's wrong now," she said, not sure if she wanted Michael to see his father this way. But it couldn't be helped. Besides, Michael had been around any number of her patients and had never gotten squeamish. Somehow, she'd always thought he might be a doctor, even though his fascination was clearly for bugs.

"Is he sleeping?" he asked, his attention suddenly caught by some computer equipment stashed in the corner of the room. It was still boxed, as was an unassembled workstation next to it.

"You dad got stung by some hornets today, and—" Ten thousand scenarios clicked through her mind as she opened her medical bag. Delayed reaction to the stings, some kind of undetected cardiac problem. "And I think he may have taken a shot that made him go to sleep pretty quickly." She hoped it was an allergic reaction to the antihistamine—the drug that should have prevented an allergic reaction to the stings.

"Paper wasps," Michael corrected. "They make paper from dead wood and plant stems for their nests." He frowned. "But they don't usually sting unless someone attacks them first."

"Did you hear that, Cade? They don't usually sting unless someone attacks them first," she said, as she unlocked the medical bag with a key she wore on a chain around her neck—a precaution since she had an active, inquisitive child in the house. Then she grabbed out an epi pen—a pen filled with epinephrine, which would, in theory, stop the allergic reaction. "Please, hand me the stethoscope," she asked Michael once the shot was in.

"Can I listen to his heart after you do?" Michael asked, even though his eyes were fixed on his dad's computers.

"Maybe. You'll have to ask him, after I wake him up." His heart sounds were good. Wheezes decreasing, the gurgles going away. Airways relaxing now.

"OK," Michael responded. "Then can I set up his computer?"

"I think that sounds like a wonderful idea," she said, not even caring that Cade might have other plans for it. Right now she had an emergency to deal with, a seven-year-old child to distract, and a brand-new computer was the best thing she could think of for her son. She glanced quickly at Michael to make sure he was OK, then right back at Cade, who was already beginning to stir. His eyes were fluttering open and he was trying to shake his head, as if to shake away a fog.

"What happened?" he whispered, rather thickly.

"Did you take an antihistamine shot?" she whispered back.

"After I came home. Couldn't get comfortable, the stinging was increasing..."

"Then I think you're allergic to the antihistamine," she said, finally allowing herself to sit in a comfortable position next to Cade rather than stooping over him. "Classic anaphylactic reaction. You responded well to epi, though." And he'd scared her to death. Jolted some feelings to the surface, too. Thoughts and feelings about her life without Cade in it somewhere. "And you're going to stay down for the next half-hour to make sure nothing else goes wrong."

"Where's Michael?" he asked, his voice finally returning.

"Putting together your computer equipment. I

thought it was a suitable reward for saving your life."

"I did?" Michael asked, not even bothering to look at his parents he was so intent on studying the laptop computer he'd already pulled from the box.

"You did," Belle said, overwhelmed by so many emotions she was suddenly on the verge of tears. "And I'm so proud of you."

"Then can I still invite Dad to dinner?" he asked, as if what he'd done had been an every-day thing.

"Yes, you can." She turned her head sway to swipe at a stray tear that had fallen. Life with-out Cade? She didn't even want to think about it, didn't want to think why she was all caught up in this emotion either. It was a scare, that's all. Just a scare. Yet when she closed her eyes and didn't picture Cade there… "If he's up to eating."

"I'll be fine in a few minutes," Cade said, reach-ing over and taking hold of her hand. "Are you OK?" he whispered.

"I'm fine. But you almost weren't, Cade. Damn it, you almost weren't." Life was so fragile. As a doctor, she saw that all the time. But as Belle

Carter, mother and ex-wife, maybe this was the first time she'd realized it in a deeply personal way. "I don't know what I'd have done if you..." Biting back the rest of her words, she held tighter to his hand as she swiped away more tears with her other hand. "Damn you, Cade Carter. Why did you do this to me?"

"What?"

Her answer was a tender kiss to his forehead. Not missed by Michael, who caught it on camera. Then came total silence. What was there to say other than the obvious? Her feelings were deeper than she'd thought. And that was something for which she had no words.

Thirty minutes later Cade felt up to eating. But more for the company than for the food. The whole ordeal had worn him out. The stings, the allergic reaction. He'd much rather have gone to bed, but he didn't want to disappoint Michael and, in a way, he wanted to be with his family for a while, even though they weren't really a family any more. Yet they were as close as it got for him, so he took a small portion of spaghetti, pushed it around on his plate, tried to force down a few bites, then looked helplessly at Belle as he pushed the plate away. "You always were a good cook."

"I never cooked," she said.

"Sure you did. Once or twice."

"And you remembered?"

"I remember the good times. We should have had more of them, then maybe I wouldn't feel so…" He glanced at Michael, who was cramming spaghetti into his mouth as fast as he could. "He's in a hurry?"

"He wants to get back up to your apartment and finish setting up your computer. Something about a router and connecting it to something else wireless." She shook her head. "I'm not sure."

"A wireless internet connection," Michael explained in all impatience, like everybody should know what he was talking about. "We can network him in with us, so he won't have to have a separate hook-up. And all I have to do is—"

"Finish your dinner," Belle interrupted. "Then your reading. Then go to bed. It's getting late, you've had a busy day, and your dad's computer can wait until tomorrow."

"But…" Michael started to protest, then stopped,

shrugged, and pushed himself away from the table. "OK. I'll go read."

"You're finished eating?" Cade asked. Michael didn't answer, though. His mind was already somewhere else, probably racing on to the next adventure or the next challenge to solve. "He's obedient," he commented to Belle.

"At times. Then at other times he's a seven-year-old tornado, like every other child his age is occasionally. You can't keep him down, he won't mind, he's sullen, gets angry..."

"Sounds like me at his age. One minute sweetness and light, then the next—boom! Except I didn't have an Einstein intelligence to go with it." He stood, stepped away from the kitchen table, and pushed his chair back in.

"Michael's the one thing we did right, Cade. Even with all our mistakes, we have an amazing son."

"I can think of a couple of other good things we did, too. But Michael's definitely the best. So anyway—I appreciate you saving my life and all, but I'm exhausted, so I think it's time to get back to my apartment and get some sleep."

Belle laughed. "You're so casual about it.

Thanks for saving my life, but…" She got up from the table, too. "Look, you've had a rough day. You deserve a real bed, so take mine. I'm good on the couch."

"You don't have to do this, you know."

"Sure I do. As your doctor, as the mother of your son—"

"As a friend?"

"Maybe. But does it ever really work when ex-spouses turn friends? Aren't there always some hard feelings buried somewhere, even though you profess an amicable divorce? So for tonight—"

"I'm sleeping in my doctor's bed. And for what it's worth, she's the best friend I've ever had."

Belle nodded, choosing to ignore the last part of that remark. "Well, your doctor didn't have time to put on clean sheets."

That didn't matter. Smelling Belle's scent on the sheets wasn't as good as having her there next to him, but it would definitely make his sleep come easier.

"One last thing. Did you know you have an antihistamine allergy? At your age, I'd have thought…"

"You thought I'd take something that would

knock me down hard enough so I'd find my way to your bed?" A huge grin spread across his face.

"You almost died," she snapped. "It's nothing to joke about."

He shrugged. "What else is there to do?"

"Take it seriously. Wear a warning bracelet. Make sure that next time you almost die, you do it somewhere where our son isn't watching." She bit her lower lip. "Damn it, Cade! You scared me. When I opened that door and saw you there, on the floor…"

He walked around the table and stopped directly in front of her. So close, he could smell the slight hint of strawberry-scented shampoo in her hair. "It's nice to know you still care—a little bit."

Holding her ground, not backing away even an inch, she looked up, met his stare. "This won't work, Cade," she said. "We won't work."

He cocked his head slightly, continuing to stare into the most beautiful green eyes he'd ever had the privilege of staring into. "They weren't who we are, Belle. Those two people back then, they were nothing like we are now."

"For once, we agree on something. But the two people who exist now are too wise for this, Cade.

They've been through too much. Can't go back, can't move forward."

"But what about right now? Sometimes living in the moment isn't such a bad thing."

She didn't respond. Just held her ground, looking at him. Searching his eyes for an answer? Or asking a question? He didn't know. Which ultimately was the reason that made him step forward to find out. And in that sweep of mere inches it was like the air between them turned into a barrier...the barrier they needed to keep them separated. They'd always been so good at this, perfect in a way he'd never known perfection, and had never found since Belle. One kiss was all he wanted. A reminder of the memory. And he could feel the barrier shifting, feel it slipping away as he raised his hand to stroke her cheek, and she leaned her face into the cup of his hand. Shut her eyes. Sighed softly. Relaxed. Smiled.

Gently, very gently, he slipped his hand from her cheek to just below her jaw, then tipped her head back, but only slightly. Just enough to see her every feature—imperfections, perfections, everything he'd loved about that face flooded back to him. This was a Belle he knew so well, yet didn't know at all. A Belle he'd never before kissed, yet could almost savor the taste of her lips without even touching them, the lingering memory of that taste was so keen.

She wasn't stopping him. But she wasn't encouraging him either. His choice, entirely, to kiss her or step back. Feel yet another sting, or avoid that next pain altogether.

No choices here, though. Not for him. He wanted her, felt it crushing hard at him as he lowered his lips to hers and awaited her verdict.

Belle's verdict... She snaked her left hand around his neck and pulled his face down to her, while the fingers on her right hand tangled themselves in his hair. That touch had always given him chills. Caused him to gasp... And as he did, as his mouth parted ever so slightly, she pressed her tongue to his, which caused fire, pure fire to ignite him like he hadn't been ignited since the night of their divorce...one for the road, she'd called it.

"Belle," he murmured against her lips as she pulled herself into him, pressed the length of her body hard into his, demanding more, demanding everything.

There was nothing tentative here. The kiss grew more carnal, lips pressing even harder, tongues plunging even deeper, no dividing lines. The feel of her fingernails digging into the flesh of his neck, the bite of reality...damn, what was he doing? A question he asked himself again as she removed her hand from his neck and squeezed it in between them, pressed it to his chest, raked it from slightly below his shoulder to his pectoral, then...pushed him back. Hot, sweaty, aroused, half-dazed, he took that step, then exhaled a shudder. "Now what?" he asked, trying not to sound as ragged as he felt.

"Nothing. We were curious. We satisfied that curiosity. One moment, and it's over. We don't have to do it again."

Maybe that's what she wanted him to believe but, oh, those eyes said something entirely different. And he'd always been able to read her eyes. "Fine. One moment." He took another step back. "If that's what you want."

"We're not reconciling, Cade. If that's why you came to Texas, go home."

"Why I came to Texas," he murmured, smiling, "was for Michael."

Once again, she didn't respond. Just stared. And it occurred to him that Belle was a little mixed up about this. A little off balance. Well, she could join the club. This was about as off balance as he'd ever felt in his life, and that included the day she'd told him the marriage was over. He'd expected that. But not this. Not any of it. "Goodnight, Belle," he finally said, struggling with the idea that there was more below the surface. And there was, he was sure of it. But he wasn't in the mood to figure out what it was. Leftover feelings, new feelings, curiosity, as she'd said. It had been a hell of a day, from the wasp stings to the anaphylactic reaction to that damned kiss. Somewhere in all that mess, though, he was sure of one thing. As rough as his day had been, his night, snuggled alone between Belle's sheets, was going to be even rougher.

CHAPTER SIX

IT WAS the unsettling feeling waking her up that something wasn't right, as well as her mother's intuition that sent her running for Michael's bedroom first, only to find an empty bed. "Michael!" Belle called out, looking in his closet then under his bed. "Where are you?"

Michael didn't turn up in the bathroom, kitchen, or den, not in her bedroom with Cade either, she discovered when she peeked in, only to find her bed was empty as well. Where had he taken Michael? Without telling her?

The panic in her fast giving way to anger, Belle looked out the kitchen window and saw the garage apartment lit up at— She glanced at the wall clock. Two in the morning! Cade had taken Michael out at two and there was no doubt in her mind they were up there assembling the computer. It was so…so irresponsible of Cade to do that, to allow it, or enable it, whichever the case turned out to be. That was the thought that propelled her up the stairs and straight to Cade's door, which she shoved open rather than knocking.

Inside, looking as innocent as you please, father and son were sitting cross-legged on the floor, both absorbed in their individual projects—Michael with the laptop, clicking away on the keys, and Cade with a screwdriver in one hand and an instruction sheet in the other. It could have been a cozy scene under different circumstances, with father assembling a knock-together desk while son assembled computer peripherals and installed software. But not under these circumstances. "You're supposed to be in bed, Michael," she said, fighting to sound patient when everything inside her was boiling mad. "You know you're never…never allowed to get up in the middle of the night and leave the house unless it's an emergency, and we've talked about those. Do you understand me?"

It wasn't Michael who responded, though. "I couldn't sleep. Got up, decided not to disturb you, and came up here. Apparently our son had been here for a while, working."

"My son knows the rules," she said, stepping

around the cartons on the floor, on her way over to Michael. When she got there, he finally looked up, picked up his camera, then clicked a picture of her, which made her even angrier, in turn causing her attempt to hold it in even more difficult. "And doing what he's doing right now is breaking one of them. So, Michael, please get up and come with me back to the house."

"But I'm almost finished," he argued, getting ready to click and shoot again. This time at Cade, though, who was putting on a properly stern face, even though his eyes were anything but stern.

"No, Michael. You are finished for tonight. Now get up and go back to the house. No arguments. Do you understand me?"

"Ten more minutes?" he asked. "That's all I need."

She didn't answer his question. Instead, she simply stood there, frowning that mother's frown every child knew, the one that told the child he'd better mind, or else. In this case, Michael knew what "or else" meant…two days without his video games. Not a cruel punishment by most parental standards, not even a harsh one, but it was effective on a seven-year-old boy who, too often, thought he should have adult privileges.

"OK," he grumbled, then stood. And snapped another picture of her, one that captured her mother's frown. "I'm going."

"Straight to bed," she said. "I'll be there in a minute to make sure that's where you are." This time she turned her frown on Cade, who was still sitting cross-legged on the floor, and her expression definitely had nothing to do with being a mother. "After I talk to your father."

"OK," he said again, then marched sullenly to the front door. But before he left, he turned back to Belle and Cade, snapped one last photo of the two of them, then stomped out the door and down the wooden steps, every last footstep sounding as loud as Michael could make them. On purpose.

"I suppose I should apologize," Cade said, pushing himself off the floor.

"I suppose you should," she snapped, her attention still centered on Michael while he stomped on across the yard and into the house. Finally, when he was in and the back door was shut, she whirled around to face Cade. "What were you thinking, Cade? Do you realize that by sitting here, aiding and abetting Michael, you've endorsed his actions? Or, at least, in his mind you have!"

"I was thinking that since my son had come up here to work on the computer in the middle of the night, I should probably stay with him since he's too young to be out here on his own, like he was."

"Did it occur to you to make him go back to bed? Or did you even remember that I'd specifically told him he wasn't going to work on the computer any more tonight?"

"Actually, I did. Then he told me that, technically, it was the morning of the next day. Not a logic I'd particularly cared to argue with him."

"In other words, he wins, I lose?" She shook her head vehemently. "Look, Cade. I know you don't get to be a full-time dad, but you can't pit Michael against me, which is what you just did. He's smarter than any kid has a right to be, and he can manipulate situations with the best of them. That's what happened here. Michael knew what he was supposed to be doing, but you're the one who caved." She took another look out the window to make sure Michael wasn't trying to sneak back, and saw that his bedroom light was on. So for now, he was on his way back to bed. She turned to Cade again. "We're in this together, and you're going to have to support me when I tell Michael to do something. If you can't, then find another place to stay tomorrow."

"You were always so sexy when you were angry, Belladonna," he said, nudging a couple of cartons away from the cot in the corner. "Still are. And for what it's worth, I'm sorry. I saw an opportunity, and took it. I know I should have made him go back to bed the second I found him here, but the excitement on his face... I don't get to see that very often. So if you want to be mad as hell at me for breaking your rules, there's nothing I can do about it. But it was worth it, and I won't do it again." He plunked himself down on the cot with a groan and turned over on his side. "Under the circumstances, I think I'll be safer spending the rest of the night out here. So now I'd like to make the most of what's left of it, because Bill Thompson is coming into the office at six to have me check his prostate and as I haven't done that kind of an exam in years, I need my sleep."

"At six?"

"Only time he could make it." He shrugged,

winced, and smiled up at her. "Oh, and he said he likes having a man back in the office."

"Well, tell him not to get used to it." Belle spun away, and headed for the door. Halfway there she turned back to Cade. "Oh, and so you'll know, I'll be locking the house doors when I go in."

"Spare key?" he asked, trying to find a comfortable position.

She watched him wince as he settled in on the cot, thought about inviting him back to her bed, then give herself a mental kick. "Nope. No spare key." For her own good. "And tomorrow I'll be having electronic locks installed. Seems Michael is being tempted by outside forces."

"Or inside," he said, then shut his eyes and let out a ragged sigh.

And that was the problem. Cade wanted in and she didn't blame him. But getting into Michael's life more than he was also meant he was back in hers, and that's what she didn't want. Truth was, there were moments when she caught herself reacting the way she had the first time she'd ever laid eyes on him. Breathless, heart palpitations, trying to be cool, even cold about it. She liked to remember it as when surgery met internal medicine. He'd been a surgical resident, she'd been a medical student assigned to a rotation through his service and had seen, right off, how five other female students had practically swooned over him. And he'd loved it. Eaten it right up.

Well, not her. Sure, there was the attraction factor, but Cade…he was like this enigma. Very perplexing and contradictory. The ultimate surgeon, skilled, passionate, devoted. Yet not settled outside his medicine. The man she might want, yet the man she was pretty sure she didn't want. Consequently, her self-imposed coolness toward him had lasted for the duration of her service under him, and she'd had to fight every step of the way to keep herself from looking as silly as the other women had when they'd been around him, because Cade certainly did have his way.

First day off of Cade Carter's service, though, he'd asked her out and she'd jumped at the chance, then all that coolness had melted into a puddle. First night—a night to remember. But the thing even more memorable was, in spite of Cade's way, he had been genuine, and nice. His charm had oozed naturally. One date, one night, she'd been hooked.

For all his faults, and there were a few she'd learned over the years, Cade had never cheated on her . He could have. Opportunities had been thrown at him all the time. Yet that first night together he'd made her that promise, and it was the one promise he never broke. Oh, he'd cheated on her with life, going in more directions than she could keep up with, and in an ambition that had simply kept getting bigger and bigger until it had squeezed her out. But as a lover, then a husband, Cade had stayed faithful—something she'd never doubted in him. Even now, she remembered, with a little smugness, how she used to walk down the hospital halls, watching all the women swooning over him, all of them envious that he was hers.

So the problem Belle was facing now was that the things she'd found irresistible before hadn't changed, and the things she'd found positively infuriating had...for the better. The Cade Carter who existed now was the man she'd hoped she was getting nine years ago. But the Belle Carter who existed now wasn't the woman who, nine years ago, had wanted Cade beyond all reason. Their happily-ever-divorced status was changing because of proximity, and there wasn't a darned

thing she could do about it. He wanted to be closer
to his son, and Michael certainly needed that. She
didn't, however. And maybe the true reason she
didn't was because, deep down, she was beginning to discover that she really did.

For whatever it was worth, and she hoped not
very much, Cade still had his way, and she was
still swayed. But wiser. And wise always won
over anything else in her life.

"Are you sure he's going to be OK?" Cade asked,
watching the bus drive off with his son.

"It's three days, and Dr. Robinson is the best."
Belle waved at the bus, even though Michael never
looked out the window to wave back. He was too
preoccupied with his hand-held electronic game.

"The best at what?"

"I already told you. She has impeccable cre-
dentials as a doctor of medicine for starters.
Pediatrics. On top of that a doctorate in psy-
chology, specializing in autism and specifically
Asperger's syndrome. Amanda's done some of
the leading research in the country and Michael
responds well to her." Smiling, Belle patted Cade
on the arm. "You've always accused me of being

the overprotective one, and just listen to you. He's going to be gone for three days, Cade. You'll survive, which really isn't my biggest concern. And Michael will have a good time, which *is* my biggest concern. But what I'm counting on most is Amanda's evaluation for progress. She's watching his social interactions, by the way. Michael's typical of the social awkwardness associated with Asperger's and that's what we've been working on lately. You know, getting him to be more outgoing."

"Don't take this the wrong way, Belle, because I'm not challenging you, but was Michael OK with this camping trip, or is it something he's doing because you insisted?" Robbie hadn't been OK any of the times he'd been sent away. In fact, he'd run off more often than Cade probably ever knew about after Cade's mother had sent Robbie packing to one program or another. Groups homes, military school, private care facilities—you name it, and that's where she'd sent Robbie. In fact, dispatching his brother's upbringing to someone else had always been her priority, because she hadn't cared. Cold, heartless woman. She hadn't cared about him, hadn't cared about Robbie...

"Look, Cade. Insisting he do things outside his comfort zone is part of the process, but there's nothing to worry about. Michael does well with Amanda and what's more important, Amanda does well with him. Probably as well with her as he does with just about anybody other than…"

"You can say it, Belle. Other than you." He knew it was true, and the truth hurt. No matter how he wanted to deny it, or argue the fine points, he was a part-time father, and part-time fathering was a kick in the gut.

"I'm sorry but, yes. Other than me. You're in and out of Michael's life every other weekend, Cade, and flying down here the way you do—you prove yourself. It's a good thing. Something most fathers wouldn't, or couldn't, do. But Michael doesn't adapt to changes in his schedule very easily, so you don't get the best of him when you're here because he's in readjustment mode for most of that time, which is difficult for him."

Everything she said was true, like it or not. Belle was the full-time parent and he was the intrusion. Still, every other weekend wasn't enough, and that's why he was here. He had to figure out how to get more, how to be more. Had to figure out how not to be resentful of what he didn't have and Belle did. And there was no denying that, at times, he was resentful as hell. He'd caused the situation, he took full responsibility, but that didn't change the way he felt. His mistakes had cost him dearly, and it was killing him. "Look, do you want to go out to dinner tonight?" he asked, totally out of the blue.

"Are you asking me on a date?"

"Can't ex-spouses have a date every now and then?"

"They can, if one of them doesn't have evening call at one of the ranches. It's probably going to be a late night."

"And you don't eat on your late nights?"

"Well, there is this little roadhouse on the way out there. Good food, loud music. You could meet me there later."

"Or drive you to your evening call and help speed things along for you."

"With everything you've been through these past twenty-four hours, you don't have to do that, Cade."

"What if I want to?" He did want to, but he wasn't sure why. Maybe to spend some time alone with her? Actually, it was quite an appealing idea, the two of them together, no one else around. It had been years, and they used to be good at it.

Belle stepped back off the curb, took one long look down the road, even though Michael's bus was long out of sight, then nodded. "Well, I've got patients scheduled all afternoon, and you've probably got a fair portion of Big Badger's male population trekking in to see you, as they won't trek to see me, so how about we play it loose? You text me when you're done, or I'll text you when I'm done, and we'll go from there." She smiled. "Michael taught me to text, by the way."

Well, at least it wasn't a firm no. "We're working in the same office, Belle."

"But texting keeps it impersonal."

That it did. And there was no mistaking that she was sending him a clear message. But as she turned and walked away from him, he pulled out his cellphone and texted her a message that clearly wasn't impersonal. *From behind, you're still the best looking woman I've ever seen.* He watched her check her text, pause like she was thinking about it, then pick up her pace back to the office. "I mean it, Belle Carter," he shouted.

"Always were, still are." It was certainly true, but he sure didn't know where he was going with it. Especially as Belle wanted none of it, or none of him.

"Three sick, seven fine. I don't get it. There's a contaminant source that's either picking or choosing its victims, or part of the population of Big Badger is involved in something the rest of the people here know nothing about. And we're not making any progress, because these people haven't eaten anything that resembles a salad." The exams were over, no one was critically ill, she'd written the prescriptions and handed out a few pill samples to tide them over until morning, and she was ready to end the day. Grab a bite to eat, go home, kick her shoes off, and spend the first night alone she'd had since she couldn't re-member when. It sounded good. No, it sounded luxurious and she was keeping her fingers crossed there would be no night emergencies. "So let's go get dinner over with, and—"

"Is having dinner with me such a chore, Belle? We used to enjoy our evenings together."

"We used to be married, and we enjoyed our

evenings together because we only got them once every couple of weeks, if we were lucky. And, no, it's not a chore. I just want to go home, be alone, and not have to worry about anything for a few hours." Belle's words were cut off by her cellphone ringing. Ten seconds later, after the blood had drained from her face, she clicked off and jumped into the truck. "Emergency in town, at the diner. One of the customers there is giving CPR…to Maudie."

"Damn," Cade muttered, on his way to the driver's side. He jumped in, hit the gas, and within a second they were on their way back to town, not sure what they'd find when they got there.

"She's healthy," Belle finally said. "Even for her age, she's strong. And normally if *E. coli* goes beyond the usual symptoms, it's on someone who's not healthy, or elderly. But Maudie is…robust."

"You're assuming it's what everybody else is getting, but maybe it's not."

He turned a sharp corner, which threw Belle almost into his lap. In fact, she was sprawled across him quite suggestively, like a woman whose only emergency was taking care of the man next to her. She extricated herself quickly from that awkward spot, although she didn't slide away from him nearly as quickly. In fact, she lingered there purposely, enjoying the way it felt pressed up against him as she was. Tingling with goose-bumps, not even trying to hide her shivers. Yes, there was a part of her that could have invited Cade back to her bed for more than just a comfortable night's sleep. She wasn't dead after all. Neither was her attraction for Cade. And she wasn't a prude. But Cade—it worried her that he might want more. Yet the thought didn't go away. "I, um…I forgot to fasten my seat belt," she said, remembering the times when she'd purposely forgotten to buckle up so she could ride this close to him, to feel his raw strength against her arm, her hip, the way she was doing now. It did send her back to the good times.

"Apparently," he said, his voice rough.

"Look, Cade. With Michael gone for the next few days, if you want to come up to the house and stay in his room…" OK, not her room. Close, though.

"Since I've got a few more weeks ahead of me here, I'm having a real bed delivered to the apartment tomorrow," he said. "But thanks for the offer.

I wouldn't mind a door key, though. In case I need to borrow a pot, or pan."

An absolute, flat-out rejection. She'd offered the room across from her bedroom, he'd chosen the room above where she parked her car. She hadn't expected that, but maybe it was for the best. Leftover longings didn't translate into anything of substance, she knew that. So did Cade. But that didn't make his rejection sting any less. "Sure, I'll find the spare and slide it under your door later on." Said as she scooted back to her side of the truck cab and fastened her seat belt for the last three miles of their trip back to Big Badger—a trip without another word spoken between them.

He hadn't meant to turn her off cold, but that's what had happened. A little bump into his lap, a little press against his arm, and sleeping across the hall from her wasn't good enough. Having Belle so close—even now, as he pulled the truck into a parking spot behind the diner, all he could see was what he'd seen so many times before. The most beautiful, the most seductive woman he'd ever met. He couldn't do that to himself. Just couldn't do it. It would drive him crazy. In fact, he was wondering now if the garage apartment was too close. Time to brace up and remember he was here to establish a better relationship with Michael, and seducing Michael's mother wasn't part of that. Even though that's exactly what he wanted to do. "Do you know if an ambulance has been called? I didn't see one out front," he said, trying to put it all out of his head.

"Ambulance service here is…difficult. The only hospital nearby is in Newman, and it's more like a glorified clinic, with a few overnight observation beds. No emergency services, actually. So if we have something serious, we call an airlift like we did before with Dean Ralston. Maudie calls an airlift." She swallowed hard. "Which I'm sure hasn't happened yet."

"You need a hospital here," Cade said, grabbing his medical bag out from behind the seat, as well as the large, portable emergency kit with extended supplies that Belle carried with her on her trek out to the ranches. "Even a small one would be better than nothing."

"We need a lot of things, but what we have is one overworked doctor who's doing the best she can and struggling to buy her medical practice from a town that can't afford to run medical services on its own. So we deal with what we have to any way possible."

She was on his heel in the diner's back door and through the kitchen. Finally, in the dining room, they were greeted by a wall of people, all standing back as one of the servers, a young girl named Judie Lawson, huddled over Maudie, not attempting resuscitation but fanning her for a lack of anything else she knew how to do.

Judie saw Belle approach and immediately scooted away.

"I could use an IV setup," Cade said, dropping to the floor as Belle opened her emergency kit and started to pull out supplies.

"As soon as I get oxygen on her." Oxygen from a small emergency cylinder she always carried with her. Maudie looked bad. Pale. Not responsive. She glanced over at Cade, who was already midway through his first assessment. Admired the way he worked so fast, so efficiently. It's what she'd seen that first day on his service, and a huge part of what she'd loved in him.

"Pulse thready," he stated. "Respirations shallow." He glanced up at Belle. "Does she have a heart condition?"

Shaking her head, Belle pulled a large-bore line from her bag, and handed it over to him. "Not that I know of. At least, she's never said anything to me." Once Cade had inserted the IV, Belle attached a bag of normal saline to it then waited for Cade's next assessment, as he was listening to Maudie's chest again.

"No changes," he said, as Belle strapped the blood-pressure cuff to Maudie's arm.

She blew up the bulb, had a listen. "Sixty over palp." Meaning, deathly low.

"Has she shown any symptoms of *E. coli*?" Cade asked, almost in a whisper. "Because I'm wondering if this is about a heart…" He stopped, and looked at the vial Belle had fished from Maudie's pocket.

"Nitroglycerine," she said, opening the vial and shaking out a pill then putting it under Maudie's tongue to dissolve. It would improve blood flow to the heart as well as decrease the work of the heart. Something that, had she taken it at the onset of her chest pain, could have prevented this. "I don't suppose she had the chance to take a pill before this happened."

"Or didn't think it was important enough."

"She's my nurse, Cade. Maudie knows that the nitro is important, but never told me she had a heart condition, and that's what has me concerned. I should have known. She should have told me." Glancing over at Cade, who was on his phone to call for a helicopter, she went on, "She likes you better than she does me. I don't suppose she mentioned it to you, did she?"

"Not a word." After giving directions to the dispatcher, he snapped shut his cellphone then had another listen to Maudie's chest. "It's not quite so erratic. Not good, but better. Oh, and the helicopter's twenty minutes out. So I think we just hold where we are with her, unless something else happens. OK with you?"

Belle nodded. "Forty minutes getting her to a hospital—that's a long time, Cade. If they want to get a clot-buster in her, we're running out of time."

He reached over and squeezed her hand. "Don't beat yourself up about this, Belle. Maudie's going to be fine."

"She should have told me, Cade. But she's like

everybody else here. They don't trust me. My own
office nurse doesn't trust me." For the first time
since she'd come to Big Badger, she was having serious doubts about staying. Nobody trusted
her, the people in town were getting sicker every
day with a contaminant she couldn't identify. And
Maudie...

"You didn't cause it, Belle." Cade squeezed
Belle's shoulder. "Give it time."

"Time," she muttered. "So why didn't you tell
me, Maudie?" she asked the unconscious woman a
couple minutes later, as she prepared to do another
blood-pressure reading. No answer, of course, not
that Belle expected one. But the reading was much
better. Maudie was stabilizing, thank heavens.
Now, if she could just get the rest of her life to
stabilize as well.

CHAPTER SEVEN

THE first thing Belle did before she even rolled out of bed was call to check on Maudie. She'd called once during the night, learned Maudie was stable. This time, though, the news was a little more grave. Maudie was on her way to have an angioplasty, due to another cardiac episode having happened shortly after Belle had called earlier. "But she's stable?" she asked the attending physician.

"She doesn't want to be sidelined," Dr. Redmond told her. "Wants to get out of here and get back to work. Overall, I'd say she's hanging in pretty well. Once we get the procedure done—"

"And this condition. Long-standing?" Belle interrupted.

"Going on to two years."

Somewhere in the middle of the night, Belle had convinced herself that it was a relatively new condition to Maudie, and maybe not talking about it had been Maudie's way of coming to terms with

it. But two years? "Well, tell Maudie I'll come up
to see her as soon as I can. And Dr. Redmond,
if there's anything she needs, or anything I can
do, call me, will you?" After she hung up, Belle
stayed flat on her back in bed, staring up at nothing in particular. An angioplasty was a common
procedure, often a preventative for bigger problems, like full-out heart attacks. Specifically, an
angioplasty opened blocked or narrowed coronary
arteries and improved blood flow to the heart.
Shortly, a small mesh tube would be placed in
Maudie's artery to help keep it open. Then soon
Maudie would be up and about, probably back to
work, on restricted duty, in a week or two.

But it wasn't the angioplasty that bothered Belle.
It was the fact that Maudie hadn't told her about
her heart condition. Which got back to the same
old thing. She wasn't being well received here. In
other words, she was buying a medical practice
in a town that didn't trust her medical services. It
was troubling, especially since she was wagering
her and Michael's futures here. More than that, it
was frustrating.

For the first time since she'd come to Big Badger,
an awful lot of misgivings about making this her

permanent home were pelting her. Even the disdain of the men hadn't caused that, but discovering how her nurse didn't trust her enough to tell her she had angina pectoris, that shook her to the core. It made her look bad, gave the people here something else for speculation. If Maudie didn't trust Dr. Carter, what's wrong with Dr. Carter?

"But I want to stay," she said, finally pushing herself up then dropping both her feet to the floor. "I like it here, it's a good place for Michael." And she wasn't a quitter. Never had been, except on her marriage, and that handwriting had probably been on the wall long before she'd said "I do." She'd just ignored it.

Well, she could ponder it all she wanted but that didn't change the fact that she needed to get up and get her day going. A trip past the mirror on her way downstairs revealed a fright. No surprise there. Mussed hair, tired eyes—she looked exactly like she felt this morning, and she didn't care. No one was there to see her and by the time she got to her office, a little dab of makeup and some artful combing would put her in order. She wanted coffee right now, though, before she started anything. Lots of it. So she trudged out her bedroom and straight into the half-naked torso she hadn't seen half-naked in years.

"Why are you in my house?" she asked, startled to find him there. "Wearing nothing but boxer shorts?"

"Decided to take you up on the offer of a nice, soft bed for a couple days since mine is delayed in arrival." He stretched, twisted left, twisted right, showing off a pretty magnificent pectoralis major. Rather than thinking how that particular chest muscle received dual motor action by the medial pectoral nerve and the lateral pectoral nerve, the way a doctor should, all she could think was, Wow! Really, just—wow!

So with that thought in her head Belle glanced down at Cade's bare toes then up at the morning stubble on his chin, taking particular care to avoid the delicious landscape along the way. But remembering it, every solid, fine-looking inch of it. Dear God, make it stop! Then, huffing out an impatient sigh when it wouldn't, she shoved on past Cade and continued down the hall. "Put some clothes on, Cade. And stay out of my way," she called back, not turning around to look at him again.

He chuckled. "You never were a morning person, and the years haven't changed that."

"When did I lose the last shred of control over my life?" she asked, as she kept on trudging, trying not to think about what she'd encountered. But the harder she tried to blot it out, the more it seeped in, leaving her to wonder where ever had he got those muscles? He sure hadn't looked like that when they'd been married. Good, yes. But not great, the way he did now.

Twenty minutes later, fully invested in her second cup of coffee and a piece of buttered toast, with Cade finally out of her visual memory, Belle was beginning to feel like herself again. Normally, her mornings meant getting Michael up and making sure he got dressed, had breakfast, brushed his teeth, combed his hair. Then sending him on his way, either to school or to stay with Virginia Ellison, who'd raised her own autistic son and loved taking care of Michael. It all worked out perfectly. Michael had a great caregiver who loved him, Virginia was happy being needed again, and Belle had amazing peace of mind with the arrangement. All that was a large part of the reason she didn't want to leave here. Everything worked out.

Damn it! Big Badger was everything she needed. Yet this morning she was still hung over with the feeling that she wasn't what Big Badger needed, and that mattered more than what she wanted, as being a good doctor here was important—to her, to Michael, to the town. But how good could she be if the people wouldn't even let her try? In the scheme of things, that might be what ended up mattering the most.

"She came through it fine," Cade said, sitting down next to her on a stool at the breakfast bar.

"What?" Belle said, glumly.

"The angioplasty. I called to check on Maudie, and the procedure went well. I mean, I thought you were worried about her and that's why you're looking so...rough." He took the coffee mug Belle had pushed away, pulled the coffee-pot over to himself and poured himself a fresh cup, with the exception of the inch she'd left in the bottom. "Is there something else going on?"

"You!" she snapped. "That's what's going on." She gave him a quick appraisal, glad to see his jeans and T-shirt, yet a little sad he hadn't joined her in his boxers. He did look good, and when all else seemed to be going sour, having a nice view first thing in the morning should have started the day off better than it was starting. But Cade was only a temporary fix, not a solution to her problems. She sighed, and scooted the plate with the last piece of toast over at him, to go along with the coffee she'd left in the cup. Once, that kind of sharing had been intimate, normal. Now it seemed wasted. "You know, my life was fine, then you showed up and now you're drinking out of my coffee cup! My coffee cup, Cade. Like you had some proprietary right to it. That's what's going on."

"It's not about the coffee cup, Belle," he said sympathetically. "Don't even think it's about me showing up here, since I've shown up a couple times a month pretty regularly since you moved down here. So care to talk about it?"

She twisted to face him. "What I'd care to talk about is why you're really here. And why now? The rest of it, why half the town refuses to let me be their doctor, why my own office nurse doesn't trust me enough to tell me she has a serious heart condition..." Belle swiped angrily at her hair, pushing it back from her face. "Those aren't questions you can answer, and since you won't answer me about why, out of the blue, you have this need to be underfoot, there's nothing to talk about. Oh, and don't tell me it's about spending more time with Michael. Because that's just your excuse, Cade. I may not have got some of the important things right about you when I fell in love with you, but I do know when you're not being honest with me."

She pushed off the bar stool, but before she could get away, Cade grabbed hold of her arm. "Look, Belle. I know you're feeling like hell over the way the town's treating you. But you're replacing a man who took care of every last one of these people for over forty years. That's a hard legacy to inherit. The town advisory board thought you could do it, though, which is why they hired you and not somebody else. So maybe some of the people here aren't lining up at your door yet, but give it time. You've only been here two months. And in another forty years, when you're retiring, I promise they won't be too accepting of the newbie coming to replace you either." He grinned. "Because they're going to find out what I found

out a long time ago. That you can't be replaced."
He let go of her arm.

"Knock off the charm, Cade. I'm not in the
mood for it this morning."

"Bad night?"

Bad morning, she thought, but didn't say it
aloud. Finding Cade in her hall, then discovering she couldn't control her feelings about him—
at least, some of her feelings—had started her
day off with a thud. Then Maudie. And the *E.
coli* outbreak that wasn't getting solved. All that
on top of some realizations about her status here
she didn't want to be realizing. Yes, it was a bad
morning all the way around, and even a peek at
Cade's magnificent muscles wasn't going to shake
that mood out of her. "I didn't mean to take it out
on you. Sorry. It's just that things are piling up
on me. And I miss Michael. That's probably the
worst of it."

"Yet you were willing to send him off to a program for three weeks?"

"Because that's what's best for him. Doesn't
mean I wouldn't be miserable, though." And
lonely, and depressed. As well as worried every
minute of every day. "It's not easy letting go. I

know he's only seven now, but I think about the time when he leaves, whether it's off to college or out to start his own life, and it…" Her voice trailed off as she visualized Michael as a grown man. Handsome, like his dad. But that look in his eyes, the one she saw every now and then— the one that said naive in the world. That's what scared her most for her son, what she worried about on those nights she couldn't sleep.

"He's going to be fine, Belle. You're going to get him ready to face the things he'll face, and you're going to help him become a man who will achieve his fullest potential." He laughed. "Dr. Michael Carter, world-renowned entomologist."

"Or Mike Carter, one of the wealthiest people in the world due to his game creations."

"Who has a bug hobby."

Belle smiled. "And parents who clip articles about him and stash them in scrapbooks." It was nice, sharing a dream with Cade. They'd done it when she'd been pregnant—talked about what their child would be when he or she grew up. Hopes and dreams. Futures to fulfill. "Remember when you wanted to name him Phineas?"

"Or you wanted to name her Calendula?"

"I did not!" she said, laughing. "It was Calen, after my mother, and Della after my grandmother. Calen Della Carter, if he'd been a girl."

"Why didn't we want to know the baby's gender?" Cade asked. "Do you even remember?"

"Because from the time I was a little girl—"

"Now I remember. It was your dream to hear the doctor say, 'Mrs. Carter, it's a—'"

"Mrs. Carter, it's a boy!" Belle supplied, shutting her eyes to recall the moment of Michael's birth and she'd heard she had a son. A perfect, beautiful little boy with ten toes and ten fingers. "Remember how loud he was, like he was angry to be here?"

"Did a man proud, to hear his son come fighting his way into the world the way Michael did." Cade exhaled an audible sigh. "Except I was late."

"Late for eighteen hours of labor and the actual birth. But you got there right after."

"Which wasn't good enough." Suddenly, the nostalgic moment turned sour, and Cade stood up then headed for the door. "I always understood why you divorced me, Belle. I was mad as hell for a long time, but I did understand. And for what it's worth, I'm sorry I made the divorce as hard on you as I made the marriage. You deserved better than anything I ever gave you."

"You gave me Michael, Cade." She smiled. "That makes up for everything." Words spoken that he didn't hear, though, because by the time she'd said them, he'd slammed out the door. Punishing himself, Belle thought. For Michael, for the breakdown of their marriage, but there was something else, and Cade was the master of keeping himself in the shadows of evasion.

"Well, the good news is, everything I treated this morning was routine." Cade was sitting at her desk, in her rolling desk chair, with his feet propped up, looking like he belonged there. "Nothing out of the ordinary for a family practice."

"Like you'd know what's ordinary for a family practice," she said, shoving him all the way to the other side of the office.

"I'll admit, it's a challenge."

"It's a challenge and you're anxious to get back to your surgical practice. No?"

"Don't sound so hopeful about my leaving. Because working in a different type of medicine gives me a brand-new perspective. I don't really mind it."

"That's not going to get you on my good side," she warned, fighting back a smile. Cade was trying so hard to get along, it was almost endearing. Too bad he hadn't tried this hard when they'd been married.

"Then tell me what will?"

"I want that date tonight. Barring unforeseen emergencies, I've got a light schedule for the rest of the day, no evening calls on any of the ranches, and you owe me. So I want to collect." OK, where had that come from? Because those spontaneous words seemed to have popped right out of her before she'd thought about the implications of her asking him out.

He straightened up in the chair, looking more than a little surprised. "To what do I owe this sudden change of heart?"

Now she wondered if she should take back the invitation. She thought about it for a moment, landing on the fact that Cade wasn't bad company. There'd been times in the past when he'd been great company. So why not? "Calling it a change of heart is pretty optimistic. Let's say that

I wouldn't mind an evening with good food, wine, and some adult conversation."

"Not to be confused with adult activity, I'm guessing."

Even though his little innuendo caused her heart to skip a beat, she didn't comment on it. "Can you still ride?"

"We're not talking a traditional restaurant, are we?"

"There's this little spot out on the Chachalaca. A bluff overlooking the plains. Not pretty like where we went camping, but you can see forever from there, and I've always wondered what it would look like at sunset." She'd gone there once to treat a ranch hand for a rattlesnake bite, and had always longed to go back. But not with Michael. He was too young, the land too rough. Too many dangers to go there alone. But with Cade? Suddenly, her heart skipped another beat, as there were different kinds of dangers involved in going there with him. But her life was so routine. No variations. No way to step outside herself, not even for a minute. And this seemed so daring. A way to shake off the routine for a little while, and simply be Belle Carter, not doctor, not mother.

Cade stood, then bowed at the waist. "Your wish is my command."

"In the meantime…" she waved her spreadsheet of patients at him "…I've got one more patient." She glanced down at the page to see who was up next. Then laughed. Mr. Brent Gilmore. A man on her list! Maybe things were beginning to look up after all.

"Michael and I come out here occasionally. He has quite a way with animals—loves horses. And the people here at Chachalaca really like Michael so we can ride any time we want. We don't get to do it often enough because of my schedule." Never enough time was the tough part about being a single mom.

"Here I am, the Texas native living in Chicago, and you, the princess of the greater metropolitan Toronto area living in Texas. How did this happen, Belle?"

"It happened when we met in San Francisco and everything changed." In one swift motion she pulled herself up onto Sally, the dappled gray mare she always rode, looking far more experienced at horseback riding than she was. "Love, marriage, child, divorce, the quest for a better life—that's how it happened."

The stallion chosen for Cade by the ranch foreman was midnight black. Stunning creature. Temperament of a pussy cat. And Cade pulled himself into the saddle like the experienced horseman he was. "Wow. I've missed this. When I was a kid, we had a couple of horses and my dad and I rode all the time. I took it for granted because it was simply part of what we did, nothing special. But it's been years and, damn, I miss Texas."

"Life moves in strange directions sometimes. My parents owned a pharmacy. I lived in an apartment upstairs with them, then in one with you. Then in a third-floor walk-up with Michael after you and I divorced. Always in a big city. I'd never even been to Texas until I moved here, but I think I'd miss it, too."

"It does move in strange directions," Cade said, patting his horse on the neck. "Speaking of direction, you lead. Because I have no idea where this perfect place is."

The perfect place. Belle thought about that as they ambled over the rocky trail for the next little while. To her, it wasn't a place so much as it was a state of mind, or even a state of being. Perfect meant being with Michael. One time it had meant Michael and Cade. And even now, when she pictured, in her mind, what was perfect, while Michael was front and center, she did catch a glimpse of Cade standing off to the side. Maybe it was habit. Maybe she'd never really taken the time to reframe her picture. Or maybe…

Cade back in the picture, and not off to the side? That was the thought she wouldn't allow in, because no matter how much it seemed right, the three of them together scared her. Could she weather another go with Cade only to find out it was wishful thinking that got her back into the position where she'd found herself the first time around? He seemed different. Seemed more earnest in wanting to settle down, yet she wasn't sure if she could believe that. Then what about Michael? What would it do to him if they did get back together and discovered nothing had really changed? Tossing Michael about in all this was the risk she wouldn't take. Refused to take. Because there was one big thing, and it was the wall she couldn't break down in Cade. There was still something on the other side. She knew it, felt it with every fiber of her being. Cade was keeping something back, and it was something that worried her. So no matter how her emotions played out here, she wasn't going to act on them because Cade had proved himself, but not enough.

It was a sad revelation. But even now, in the middle of her life without him, Cade had set the course and like she'd been doing for the past near-decade, she followed it. Only now their roads divided, and she had her own to take. Her choice, yes. But in so many ways his choice as well. After all, he was the one who'd constructed the divide.

OK, the logical arguments were all firmly rooted, her defenses were up. Her choices. This time the shots were hers to call. So why did she feel so sad about it?

Because she still loved him. That's why. You loved who you loved, and there was no getting over it. No getting over Cade. But she could get past him, and that's what she had to do. Only how?

That was the question for which she didn't have an answer. And for the first time since she'd moved here, Big Badger, Texas, didn't seem far enough away from Chicago to save her. "So the view isn't what I'd call stunning, but what amazes me about this place is how far you can see. I'm a city girl, the farthest I've ever been able to see in my life is the next street over. But look at this, Cade. It's like it never ends out there. If you go as far as your vision will take you, you'll drop off the edge." Sort of the way she'd been feeling these past few days—dropped off the edge.

Here they were, standing on the bluff, preparing for a simple picnic, and he was actually nervous, looking out over the barren landscape with Belle, because all he wanted to do was watch her. It was like he couldn't get enough of her. That's the way it had been the first time he'd ever laid eyes on her. She'd been loitering in the back of a pack of a dozen or so fourth-year medical students, hanging on his every word, gawking at the medical machines, so enthralled—and not the way the other women in the group had been enthralled. They'd been caught up in him. Belle had been caught up in what he'd been teaching, which was what had caught him up in her. She'd wanted his knowledge, his experience. Every last scrap of it. And there he'd been, a little more than cocky because he was used to the way the other women reacted to him. Sure, he liked to think he'd been impervious, or aloof, or too dedicated to notice that kind of attention. But he was human. He'd not only noticed, he'd enjoyed.

Then there had been Belle, the one who hadn't been affected. A challenge to him, because she'd had this purpose, and it had showed on her in everything she did, turning those six weeks of working with that bunch of students into the longest six weeks of his life, trying to hold back.

No, he'd never dated students, never dated nurses he worked with, never dated colleagues. Actually, truth be told, he'd rarely ever dated, and definitely never got himself involved in anything more than a temporary situation—temporary and blessedly short. With Belle, though, he'd wanted her to look at him the way the others did. Wanted to break his own rules, ask her out, worship at her feet, whatever. Some of it had been because of her looks. Who was he kidding? She was the most drop-dead gorgeous woman he'd ever met. But she was more than looks, and as the days had gone on, he'd discovered that most of his leanings toward her had been because of her determination. Belle had been strong, she'd kept her head no matter what had been going on around her, and she had been smarter than just about any medical professional he'd ever met. Yet so…unobtainable.

So he'd spent six frustrating weeks knowing that, at the end of them, she'd rotate onto another service and he'd be a thing of the past. On that last day, though, he'd decided to give it a shot. She'd say yes, she'd say no. Either way, he had to know.

And did he find out! Then gone on to totally destroy his life and lose the best thing that had ever happened to him. "Life does seem much simpler out here, doesn't it?" he asked.

Belle turned to face him. "We usually make our own complications, Cade. If we want it simple, we can have it simple. If we want it complicated, it's ours to complicate."

"I could take that as an accusation, you know."

"And I could intend it as one, because you did complicate my life a long time ago, but it's really just a statement of fact. Or perspective. Anyway, I've brought a simple picnic, some cheese, fruit, crusty bread, wine. Not your everyday Texas fare, but if you'd like to get the blanket from my saddlebag and find a nice place for us to eat—"

"What's your perspective, Belle?" he asked, interrupting. "What's your perspective of you, me? Of us?"

"That's an odd question. I'm not sure you've ever asked me about, well, anything that matters to me. I mean, maybe you might have asked early on in our relationship, but if you did it got covered up by so many other things that I don't remember."

"We got covered up by so many other things," he said. "And I regret it."

"What's done is done. We didn't survive, and maybe that's my perspective. We didn't survive but I did, and I don't cry myself to sleep at night over things that will never be. Life moves on and you've got two choices—move with it, or let it go on without you. Michael's the one who shows me that every day. It's tough for him, being different, and so much of the time I see him trying to swim upstream. Kids tease him, he doesn't fit in for a number of reasons, yet he moves with it every day, facing the fight with a strength I don't understand, and couldn't duplicate if I tried. Our little boy is seven, with a lifelong condition that will carry him to amazing places and limit him in ways most people can't understand, and I survive every day because of him, because of what I see in him." She swiped a tear from her cheek. "That's my perspective, too. It's not simply one thing. It's—it's everything."

Without saying a word, Cade walked straight over to Belle and pulled her into his arms. She went willingly, and pressed herself to him the way she'd done all those years ago. He'd missed it, missed the feel of her, missed the emotional intimacy in such a simple thing. And he wanted it back. Wanted Belle back. Wanted his family back.

But how? Wanting something and knowing how to get it were two separate things. He wanted more deeply than he'd ever wanted in his life. Even so, he was further away from having what he wanted than he'd ever been in his life. And maybe that was because he was only just now beginning to understand how much he'd lost. Yet through his loss it was obvious Belle had gained so much. So he was the one to release her, to head for his horse, to find the picnic blanket. But before he reached it, his cellphone rang. Belle's rang at exactly the same time, and they both clicked on, listened…

"I'm on my way," she choked, looking at Cade,

who was already looking up, waiting for the helicopter.

"A couple of the men from the Chachalaca are on their way out to pick up the horses," he said to her, then turned his back to speak quietly to Amanda Robinson on his cellphone. "How bad is it?" he asked urgently.

"Bad," she replied. "I sent him in by ambulance, and I'll be on my way as soon as I make sure the rest of the kids here in the camp are taken care of. But I think you'll be there before I get there."

The whir of the rotors overhead caused him to look up again. "Thanks." He clicked off the call, turned his back to Belle, and made another quick phone call, then went over to Belle and took her hand. "Dr. Robinson sent the helicopter. She called your service, they told her where we were," he shouted, as they ran to the flat stretch beyond the bluff, while the pilot sat the chopper down in a whirlwind of dust and waited for Cade and Belle to climb on board so he could take them to the hospital, where Michael had been admitted a while earlier, displaying the classic signs of *E. coli* infection, but with serious complications.

"I've been on the phone with the hospital. He's

already there and they called for my permission
to—to put him on dialysis, Cade," Belle managed
to say as she strapped herself into the helicopter
seat. "He's not…"

Cade strapped himself in next to, motioned for
the pilot to take off. "Your Dr. Robinson caught
it early, Belle. She recognized the symptoms."

"But he would have been sick when he went
with her."

"Showing no symptoms."

"No symptoms, Cade? He never complains
about anything. I sent him to school with a
hundred-degree fever one day and didn't even
know that he had a virus. The school nurse caught
it because he was eating ice—ice to cool himself
down. I'm a doctor, and I didn't even see that my
own son was sick. And with this…" She visibly
shuddered, then wrapped her arms around herself.
"Everybody here's getting sick and I've been too
concerned about saving some cows to do what I
should have…"

Cade grabbed hold of Belle's arm and gave her
a gentle shake. "Stop it!" he ordered. "You're not
doing yourself any good taking the blame, and
it's certainly not going to help Michael if you're

in such a bad emotional state when he sees you in a little while."

"Sees me? He's not going to see me, Cade. Michael was admitted unconscious. The emergency doctor said he was so sick he went into a coma right after he got there, and I'm not there to..." Tears streamed down her face, and she sniffled. "To hold him when he needs me."

Cade tried putting his arm around her, but she shoved him away.

"Don't," she snarled. "Just—don't!"

"That's right. You're the one who gets to be the martyr, aren't you? Just shove me away and take it all on your shoulders."

"How dare you? You weren't even in the country when Michael was diagnosed with Asperger's syndrome. In fact, I didn't even know where you were. Hadn't heard from you in three weeks."

"I was in Cambodia, working in an amputee clinic. You knew where I was, if you'd wanted to call me. Or e-mail."

"In Cambodia. Did you ever tell me where, exactly? Did it ever occur to you that I couldn't call you there, or that e-mails didn't go through? It went both ways, Cade. You knew where your wife and son were if you'd wanted to call or e-mail them."

"And you punished me for it, Belle. Didn't tell me for weeks that my son had been tested for autism. No, you kept that to yourself, like I didn't have a right to know. Like I didn't love my son as much as you did."

"I was angry. I didn't want to deal with…you. With anything." She shut her eyes and laid her head back against the seat, allowing the jarring from the choppy ride to divert her emotions, past and present. "I know you love him as much as I do," she finally admitted. "But it always hurt, Cade, being so alone. You had the right to know, but I hated you for abandoning me when I needed you, and I was angry at God for Michael's diagnosis, and angry at myself for all the things I couldn't control. Like now, I'm so damn angry I don't know what to do. It's not fair." She balled fists and pounded her knees. "None of it is and I wasn't there to…"

"I'm scared, too," he said, taking her balled fist into his hand and holding on for dear life. "And there's something I need to tell you now. Something I should have told you years ago, when we met, or when we married. But I didn't, and I'm apologizing now, because we can't fight about it with Michael so sick."

She drew in a ragged breath. "What you're about to tell me. Is that why you're really here?"

"No. I'm here for Michael. But it's—it's complicated."

"How, Cade?"

"I've asked someone to come help us. Called before we got on the helicopter. He's a public health doctor who's pretty much burned out for the moment. Taking this part of his life off. Spending most of his time now on a fishing boat, anchored at dock off the east coast of Texas, not fishing. But he's brilliant."

"And your brilliant, burned-out friend can help us how?"

"He's worked in some pretty difficult regions in the world, in the middle of some rough outbreaks—Africa, South America. He knows what to look for with something like the *E. coli* going around in Big Badger, and better than that he knows how to look. We need to find the source, need to find out how Michael…" He swallowed hard. "We can't protect Michael from it now, but we have to protect other children, protect everybody in town."

"You friend, if he's left medicine, then how, or why—?"

Cade held up his hand to stop her. "Jack may have some different insight into treatment as well, because that's what he does. He'll know what's best for Michael."

"You'll trust our son to this acquaintance of yours?" she snapped.

"Not to an acquaintance, Belle. To Michael's uncle."

She shook her head. Tried to process what he'd just said. "Michael's uncle? What are you talking about, Cade?"

"Something I should have talked about years ago."

"A brother? You have a brother? How could you not tell me, Cade?" She was too stunned to be angry.

"Half brother. We're estranged. Have been for a decade or more."

"Oh, so being estranged makes it all right, not telling me that my son has an uncle?"

"It's complicated, Belle. And now's not the time to get into this."

"Apparently, all those years we were married weren't the time either, were they? *Oh, Belle, by the way, let me tell you about my brother.* But it's so typical of you, isn't it? Excluding me from pretty much every aspect of your life?" Another case of someone not trusting her enough. The others were frustrating, but this one hurt. Except she couldn't process it now, let alone deal with it. So she twisted away from Cade and stared at nothing.

"He's on his way," Cade said, despite her withdrawal. "Going to meet us at the hospital. And so you'll know, he's not sociable. Probably not even friendly. But I want him working on Michael."

"Then I'll have to trust you on that, won't I? Trust being the key word here since apparently I'm expected to give it even though I don't get it from the people who matter in my life." Belle huffed out an annoyed breath. "You haven't changed at all, Cade. I thought, maybe— You know what? It doesn't matter what I think. To you, it never did."

"You're wrong," he said, almost under his breath.

She batted at the tears streaking down her

cheeks. Angry tears mixed with tears of fear. "How can I not be wrong, Cade? Tell me, because I'd like to know when, in our marriage, something about me ever mattered to you."

"It was never you, Belle. I promise, the problem was never you."

"That's not good enough, because I was the one left alone, and left out. And you were the one who left me alone and left me out of God only knows what." She drew in a ragged breath then turned to him and saw the most excruciating agony on his face. It was a pain far deeper than anything she could cope with at the moment, so she turned away and thought about Michael, only Michael, for the rest of the ride.

Minutes later, as they exited the helicopter and prepared to face whatever they had to, Belle grabbed Cade by the arm and stopped him from running straight through the emergency-room doors. "We've got to stop this," she said to him. "The *E. coli*, we've got to stop it. Tell your brother, when he gets here, that he'll have access to anything he needs in Big Badger. And if he has treatment to recommend for Michael, I'll listen."

"We'll listen. Don't shut me out of this, Belle."

"It hurts, doesn't it?" she said, then let go of his arm and ran through the hospital doors.

Cade didn't go in right away, though. As much as he wanted to, Belle was right. It did hurt being left out. But that had been his choice, hadn't it?

"He looks like you," Jack said, stepping up to the observation window going into Michael's intensive-care room. "Better looking. Could pass for Robbie's twin, I think."

Cade spun to his brother. "This isn't about Robbie!" he snapped.

"No, it's about my nephew. Otherwise not speaking to you for another decade would have been my pleasure." He stepped around Cade, pulled a stethoscope from his pocket, and headed toward the door. "Mind if I have a look at him?"

Rather than answering, Cade waved him ahead, then followed him into the room.

Belle looked up, but not at Cade. "You would be Jack Kenner, wouldn't you?"

"And you would be my ex-sister-in-law. The one I never knew I had."

Rather than answering, Belle did a quick assessment—large man, close to Cade's size. But there was no resemblance beyond that. Black hair. Dark brown eyes that saw no laughter. A mouth that never curved into a smile. Striking, but severe. Startlingly handsome, and with the same sadness or distance she saw in Cade's eyes from time to time. "Belle Carter," she said, standing then extending a hand to him. "And this is your nephew, Michael."

Jack stepped to the bedside, then simply stared down for a moment. Not breathing, not moving. Just looking. And Cade knew why. The resemblance to Robbie at that age was startling. He didn't notice it so much because he saw Michael on a regular basis and to him Michael looked like Michael. But to be confronted by the past in such an immense way, the way Jack was now, Cade felt bad for him. One more thing to add to the list. "He's had dialysis. They haven't figured why he went downhill so fast, but he's stabilizing."

Jack nodded. Drew in a ragged breath. "Any sign the kidneys are starting to kick in yet?"

"Not yet," Belle said.

Jack turned to face Belle. "Would you mind if I examine him?"

"I'd appreciate it. When Cade told me—"

"You didn't know I existed, did you? Married to the man, and he never bothered to tell you about us?"

She glanced over at Cade, whose full attention was devoted to Michael. "I expect Cade has his reasons," Belle said, surprised that she was defending Cade, and even more surprised that she wanted to defend him.

"You're one of them?" Jack asked. "Even after you're divorced?"

"One of whom?"

"The legions who fall at his feet."

"Actually, Jack, I was the legion who married him and had his child. And while it's none of your business, I want you to know that I don't fall at anybody's feet. Not Cade's, not yours. Nobody's."

Jack's answer was a low whistle and the slight arching of his eyebrows.

Admiration? Probably not. In all likelihood he was thanking the Fates he hadn't been the one to marry her, Belle decided, suddenly quite pleased with herself. "Oh, and I appreciate you coming to help. Cade speaks highly of your skills—"

"I don't give a damn what he speaks highly of," Jack interrupted, putting his stethoscope earpieces in. "I wanted to help the kid. We may not be blood, but…"

"What do you mean, not blood?" she gasped.

A sly smile crept to Dr. Jack Kenner's lips. "Seems my brother hasn't told you something else." With that, he bent down over Michael and placed the bell to his chest. "Now, if you two will excuse me, I want to make this between Michael and me. I'll let you know when I want you back in the room."

"You're kicking me out?" Belle snapped.

"Not kicking you out so much as asking you to leave. I don't need all the negative energy in here while I'm trying to get to know my nephew. And you and Cade have enough negative energy going to melt the polar ice caps all the way from Texas."

Belle swallowed hard, then stood and bent over Michael, kissing him tenderly on the cheek. "I'll be right outside in the hall," she whispered to him. "Your Uncle Jack has come to have a look at you, Michael. He's a very good doctor and he's going to take care of you." She kissed him again, then righted herself and marched out of the room, straight past Jack, straight past Cade, who followed her out, then took his place next to her at the observation window.

"How is he not related to Michael, if he's your half brother?" she muttered at Cade.

"My mother married Gerald Kenner after she and my father divorced. Jack is Gerald's son, and my mother adopted him, making him my half brother legally, no blood relationship."

"You have a mother? Since you never talked about her, I always assumed— No, you know what? It doesn't matter what I assumed. This is all about Michael, and the rest of your secrets simply don't matter to me."

"Not secrets, Belle."

"How is the presence of another family I knew nothing about not a secret? Oh, wait! It's complicated, isn't it?"

"Do you want it now?" he asked. "The short version? Because it starts with a bad mother, who didn't want to be stuck with a lower-middle-class domestic life, so she left my dad and me, married up, got everything she wanted. Because that's it, Belle. My mother walked out. Said she didn't want to be saddled with—well, for starters, me. I heard her say that. 'Why do I have to be saddled with him?' Then she traded me in for a son who at least came with a pedigree and an old man with lots of money and status. So the reason I never mentioned it is because—what was the point?"

"I'm sorry," she said, her voice low. "You didn't deserve that, Cade, but I still don't understand…" She shifted her focus back to Michael, and to Jack, who'd sat down next to the bed, taken care of Michael's hand, and was simply talking to him. "Does he have children?"

"No. Never married. But he loves them."

"I can see that." She turned to Cade. "Look, for what it's worth, I'm glad you brought him here. Whatever you two have going between you doesn't matter, at least not right now. But I want to know, Cade. At some point, I want to know everything, because it's about Michael, too. His right to know. And I'll try and keep my ego out of it since—"

"I was wrong," Cade interrupted. "About every-thing. And I'm sorry, Belle. For more than you know." With that, she went back to sit at Michael's bedside, while Jack left the room and took his place in the hall next to Cade.

"You said your mother married up," Jack said,

stopping at the window and looking back in. "I think you did, Cade. Belle deserved better than you."

"Finally, we agree on something. So, what about Michael?"

"Holding his own. Vital signs are stable, I'm cautiously optimistic that once we get the *E. coli* cured his kidney function will return. I've seen it happen like this before, seen good outcomes at the end of it. No reason to think otherwise for Michael."

"Thanks, Jack. For everything. After, well— after Robbie, I wasn't sure."

"Like you said, this isn't about Robbie. So tell me, what kind of an idiot would let someone like your amazing country doctor get away? Oh, that's right, I already said idiot, didn't I? Which answers my question."

Cade chuckled. "I'd like to say it's good to see you, Jack, but it's not." His brother looked good, though. Rugged. A little tired. He certainly had a weathered look about him, one Cade didn't remember. But it had been ten years, and Jack had still been soft back them, struggling through medical school, struggling with Robbie's death. Time changed people. On the outside time had been good to Jack, but on the inside Cade didn't have a clue.

"You always were brutally honest, except about the things that counted."

"Want to go grab a beer?" Cade asked, for a lack of anything better to offer his brother. "There's a little pub across from the hospital, and right now I think Belle would be glad to get rid of the both of us."

"Sure. Why not? Then we can sit and look at each other across the table while we're not indulging in old memories."

"I sit at the bar. The only thing I'm going to look at is the TV above the bar."

"If that's the case, I'm in. And you're buying. It's the least you can do for interrupting my fishing."

"Fishing?" Cade quipped, as they headed off together down the hall.

Belle watched them from the door to Michael's room, wondering what the real story was.

While Cade and Jack were definitely not together, they weren't exactly apart either. Strange, she thought, going back to the chair next to the bed. Definitely strange. But, then, what, about her life lately hadn't been strange?

He'd been standing there for about an hour now, looking in on Michael, while Belle sat at the bedside, holding Michael's hand. Trying to figure out a way to approach her, or just to be part of that family. It's all he wanted. And everything he'd screwed up. One screw-up compounded by another.

"You're not in there?" Jack asked.

"I was. We've decided to take turns. She'll sit with him a while so I can rest, then I'll go in while she rests."

"Well, isn't that just the united front Michael's going to want from his parents when he wakes up?" Jack snapped.

Cade turned slowly to face his brother. "If I weren't so damned angry about things that matter, I'd take offense, maybe even pound your face in the way I did that day when you accused me of taking money from your wallet."

"But you did, didn't you? Twenty bucks. That you never paid back, by the way."

"That's beside the point. We were sixteen, it didn't count."

"Michael's hanging in there, Cade. The drug I managed to procure is working."

"How did you get it, Jack? It's still in clinical trials."

"Showing amazing results. Michael's going to be one of those results."

"But nobody can just get a clinical trial drug because they want it." Except, perhaps, his brother. "And I read that it's the most expensive drug ever manufactured. So give."

"Favors. I was owed, I collected. And if the European trials weren't so overwhelmingly successful, I wouldn't have. That's all there is to say, except Michael's primary-care physician is encouraged by Michael's progress. He's got urinary output again, which means his kidneys are working. His vital signs are still stable. He's unconscious, but that's because his body is fighting hard to throw off the infection. All of which means it's time for me to head out to Big Badger to see what the hell you've got going on there. And I wouldn't be leaving Michael if he wasn't doing better." He put his arm around Cade's shoulder and, surprisingly, Cade didn't shrug it off. "Look, I'm going to go in there for a few minutes and talk to Michael before I leave. And for what it's worth, if Belle needs me to see a few patients while I'm in Big Badger—"

"See patients? And just when I'd convinced her there's nothing redeemable in you."

"For you, there's not. But I've got a nephew who needs his parents to be here, so I've got to make that happen." He stepped away from Cade. "Now go get yourself a cup of coffee, and drag her with you, if that's what it takes." He nodded to Belle, who'd barely moved, even to switch positions, in the last hour. "I'm going to sit with him for a while and hope to God you two will go off somewhere and work out whatever it is you have to work out, because I sure as hell don't want my nephew waking up in the middle of it."

Cade sighed heavily, then nodded. "Just give me a minute with her, OK? She's not doing very well with this."

"And you are?" Jack asked, his voice uncharacteristically full of concern.

"Doesn't matter what I am, does it?" He stepped back from the observation window, then turned and walked into the room. But at the door, he stopped. Didn't turn to face Jack. Just stopped and lingered there as if he was thinking. "At some point, I think you and I need to talk."

Said to the air, though, because when he finally looked at Jack, Jack was on his way to the nurses' station.

"It's time to take a break," he said to Belle, stepping up behind her. "Jack said he'd like to sit here alone with Michael for a while and talk to him. So as soon as he gets back, how about we go get some coffee, or something to eat if you're hungry?"

"Not hungry," she said. "But I wouldn't mind stretching my legs if Jack wants to stay here for a few minutes." She looked up at Cade, "Look. In the helicopter, all those things I said—"

He shook his head, then forced a smile. "Don't remember you saying anything." Raising his hands to her shoulders, he began a gentle knead. "It's a lot to deal with, and nothing really counts but Michael getting better."

She melted into his touch. Relaxed for the first time in hours. "How could this have happened, Cade? I'm careful. Even though nothing I've had

tested came back positive, I washed everything…
double-washed. And now—" Her voice broke.

"He's holding his own right now. That drug Jack
got hold of is working."

"Which isn't enough. He needs to be improving. Has to be improving." She twisted around to
face him. "He's had dialysis, Cade. His kidneys
are better now, but what if—what if Jack hadn't
been able to work his miracle? And what am I
going to do about the people in Big Badger? They
need me, too, but I can't leave my son to go take
care of them."

Cade stepped around to face her, then bent
down. "Shh," he said, reaching out and taking
hold of both her hands. "It's all taken care of.
Jack's going back there in a little while, and he's
going to manage the practice for you."

"He'd do that?"

"His idea. Something about Michael needing
us both here."

"He's a good man, Cade. I'm not even going to
ask how he got the trial drug because I don't care.
He did. That's all that matters. I didn't like him
at first, and I was wrong. You are, too, if you still
hate him. And while I don't know what's wrong

between you two, you and Jack should…" She
glanced over at Michael, studied the rise and fall
of his chest. He was on oxygen, not a ventilator, so
even that small movement reassured her Michael
was still with her, even if, right now, the condition
of his young body had taken his mind to another
place. For safekeeping, was what she told herself.
Michael's gone someplace for safekeeping. "You
and Jack and Michael should spend time together
as a family. Maybe go camping when Michael's
up to it because he's going to need it, need that
solidarity. I think Jack can be important to him.
But I also think he can be important to Jack."

"You two ready for a break?" Jack asked from
the doorway. His attention wasn't fixed on Belle
or Cade, however. It was undivided, and only for
Michael. "Because Michael and I've got some
things to talk about." He walked over to the bed
and looked down. Studied him for a moment, then
nodded. "Lots of things, don't we, Michael?"

"Cafeteria?" Cade asked, once they'd left the
room.

"I'd rather take a walk in the garden, if you don't
mind. Step outside the hospital for a few minutes,
breathe some real air. It gets a little confining in

there." Instinctively, she looped her arm through Cade's the way they'd used to do when they'd been married. Back then it had been for the connection. She hadn't been able to get enough of him. Today, it was for the physical support because she wasn't sure her legs would carry her where she wanted to go. "Maybe on the way back in we could stop by Maudie's room for a minute. I hear she's going to be released tomorrow, and she's been sending messages, asking about Michael."

"She's really concerned, Belle."

"You saw her?"

"For a minute. She called me, so I ran upstairs to look in on her, and she's the same old Maudie. Loud, demanding, heart of gold. They've adjusted some of her medications, and she's going to be cleared for light duty in a week. Full duty in about a month—if you want her back."

"If I want her? What's that about? I never, ever said anything about—"

"She's past retirement age, Belle. That's why she didn't tell you about her heart condition. It wasn't because she didn't trust you. She was afraid that with her angina, on top of her age, you wouldn't want her as a nurse. That you'd hire someone half her age if you found out about her medical condition."

"Why would I want someone with half her experience? How would that be of benefit to my medical practice?" She breathed out a ragged breath. "Why didn't she ever tell me any of this, Cade? Am I that unapproachable?"

"It's not you, Belle. It's because it's not easy admitting our deepest fears, or talking about the things that hurt us most. Maudie doesn't need the income, she needs to be needed, and you're the one who has the power to change her life, to turn her into someone who's…unnecessary."

"So she'll talk to you and not to me. That's not the way it's supposed to work. But apparently I'm wrong about that. Nobody talks to me. Not you, not Maudie… Michael didn't even tell me he wasn't feeling well. I'm his mother, Cade, and he didn't—"

"Does it make it all better, torturing yourself this way?" he asked. "Because you can blame yourself over and over, say exactly the same words every time you do, but that won't change anything. Michael's sick, it's not your fault. You're not a bad mother because your son didn't tell you he was sick. And who knows, maybe he wasn't. Sometimes the symptoms hit so hard and fast you don't feel them coming on. Especially with some of the new strains of *E. coli* coming on the scene."

Moving through the garden, through the patches of prickly pear cacti blooming in various shades of yellow and gold and past the rows of lavender prairie verbena, they came to stop under a trellis draped with Carolina jasmine with its yellow blooms, and Confederate jasmine with its darker leaf and white blooms. The sight was magnificent but the scent... Belle shut her eyes and simply breathed it into her lungs, into her soul. "It would be nice, having a small hospital in Big Badger. One with a garden like this," she said, as she sat on the marble bench underneath the trellis. "Then people like Michael and Maudie wouldn't have to be so far from home when they're sick. Except Big Badger can't even really support a medical practice. If it weren't for the work I get from the ranches..." She paused, took in another deep, perfumed breath, then shook her head. "But none of that's important right now, is it? I should stay focused on Michael. Try to figure out if there's more I could be helping him with."

"You're giving him every bit of strength you have, Belle. That's all you can do."

"Is it?" she snapped. "If I hadn't brought him here to Texas, if I hadn't been trying so damned hard to prove that I could be as—as good a doctor as you are, then he'd be fine. But no! I had to up-root him from Chicago, move to a place I'd never even seen." She swiped at angry tears. "You don't know, Cade. You—you can't understand how I'm feeling right now. I'm so—"

"Numb?" he asked. "And angry, and scared? You want to hate someone, or something, but you don't know what or who? And if there were a wall in front of you, you'd like to put your fist through it, or kick through it, or fall against it and cry. Or run away? Or go to bed, pull the blankets up over your head, and pray you're not trapped in a nightmare? Most of all, you despise yourself for what you didn't see or know, or what you didn't do? And your heart is ripping in half, hurting so bad that you're not sure it's going to give up its next beat? Is that how you feel, Belle?"

She looked up at him, blinked back her tears. "I'm sorry, Cade. I know I'm not the only one who's feeling…" She shrugged.

"Well, you do come out of it the other end, Belle. For what it's worth, I've read to the back of the book already, and while I can't predict the exact detail of the plot, I do know the overall premise and you do get through it. You have to. There's not another choice."

It was said so bitterly it scared her. Even at his worst, Cade had never sounded like this. He was scared to death about Michael, but this cut deeper. She could sense it in him. "The exact detail is where Michael gets better. That's what I have to believe because it's all I can believe. But what you said…" She paused, drew in a deep breath, and braced herself. "This isn't about Michael, is it?" This was the rest of the story, something to do with Cade and Jack, something to do with why Cade was here. And it was a painful story. She could feel that even though Cade had yet to speak. "Please, tell me about it now," she encouraged.

"There's nothing to tell because everything's about Michael! My son is lying in there, in the medical intensive-care unit, fighting for his life."

"But the book you read the back of wasn't Michael's, or even mine." She drew in a shuddering breath. "Whose was it, Cade? Don't shut me out this time, because I have to know."

"Nothing I can tell you will make things better for Michael," he said, stepping out from under the trellis but not leaving. His back was to her now, he was staring off into a patch of tall pampas grass, looking at nothing, seeing nothing but his own misery. "I'd give my life for him, Belle. You've got to believe that. If Michael needed a healthy, beating heart, I'd rip mine out and hand it to them to put in him."

"I know you would," she said, walking up behind him, wrapping her arms around him and laying her head against his back. "But, Cade, you've still got to tell me. Maybe it won't help Michael, but it will help me help you, and he needs you right now—all of you, all of your strength. And you're torn. So for Michael…" At the mention of their son's name, she felt Cade's shoulders slump. Heard him draw in the ragged, tearful breath that finally, when it left him, would leave with the words he needed to say, the words she needed to hear. "Whose book, Cade?" she repeated.

"Robbie," he said. "My younger brother—by

blood. Four years younger. Jack's younger brother, by blood, too."

There might have been a time when Cade revealing yet another secret would have made her angry, but not now. The rest of the words didn't matter, because she knew. "Your mother had a child by your stepfather."

He nodded. "Her way of trying to hold on to him, I suppose. And since she was such a good mother to the one she'd already had, as well as the one she'd adopted, why not? Except Robbie—he wasn't like Jack or me. He was…" His voice faded away off as he turned to face her. Then he drew in a bracing breath. "Robbie was autistic, Belle."

This was something she hadn't expected, and she bit down hard on her lip to keep from gasping. "Was it Asperger's syndrome?" she finally managed to ask.

Cade shook his head. "Kanner's syndrome. Robbie didn't connect to people. Certainly not to my mother, not even to his father. He was very much in his own little world, wanted everything to be the same all of the time. Wore the same clothes every day, ate the same food. Robbie was such a sweet little boy, Belle. Yet overall he wasn't very high functioning, and my mother hated that because Robbie made her look…bad. Made her look like a failure in her social circle. She hated it so much that she'd lock him in his room all day when he was home, so she didn't have to deal with him. And she was always sending him away to some sort of institution or program…"

Belle gasped. "Amanda's program. That's why you'd never talk to me about it. You did remember, though, didn't you? And you came here to prevent me from sending Michael because of the way your mother always sent Robbie. But why couldn't you tell me, Cade? Didn't you think I'd listen, or be sympathetic enough?"

"Robbie liked his world simple, and orderly, and that's all he wanted," Cade went on, seeming not to hear Belle. "Except…" He swallowed hard. "Attention from his older brothers. He craved Jack's and my attention."

Cade stepped away from her and returned to the bench underneath the trellis, where he finally sat down. "He loved Jack and Jack was so good with him. Took time, never turned him away. But me… it was never simple, and that's why I couldn't tell you. Because I did things I couldn't even admit to myself, let alone speak out loud."

"To Robbie?" She didn't know what to think yet, except she trusted Cade. No matter what he said, or thought, she trusted him and she was going to hold on to that.

He nodded. "To Robbie. See, the thing was, I didn't want to go visit my mother. Never wanted to visit her when it was her weekend to have me. Or her holiday. I fought to get out of it, but my dad always insisted I had to do the right thing. I mean, I knew the only reason dear old Mom even let me inside her house was for appearances, and the more I was forced to be around her, the angrier I got. The angrier I got, the more I resisted. And poor Robbie—he simply got caught in the crossfire. I think because I wasn't there most of the time, when I was, he wanted so much from me. Just time and attention, really. But I couldn't give it the way he wanted and I always looked for ways to avoid him, avoid the whole damned situation involving my mother."

The end to this story was something she wasn't going to want to hear. She was sure of it, and her heart was already starting to break, even though she didn't know why. But she'd started this, and there was nothing she could do to stop it, so she returned to the trellis and sat down beside Jack, taking care to keep her distance. His body language was rigid now, which meant he was rejecting sympathy, physical or otherwise. "Go on," she encouraged, glancing over at the hospital, wondering how Michael was. Surely Jack would come get her if Michael's condition changed? Still, she was nervous being away from him this long. Yet she couldn't get up and walk away from Cade now, and leave him here like this. "Tell me what happened."

"What happened was that Robbie never changed. He was always this sweet, innocent little kid who couldn't wait to see me. Year after year, that's just the way it was. But my mother hated him, the way she hated everything but her so-called status. And the older Robbie got, the bigger he got. It wasn't so easy to keep him in his room any more, and most of the places she sent him sent him right back to her because Robbie wandered off, and they didn't want to assume any responsibility for that.

"So, one Christmas. I was seventeen, Robbie was thirteen. And living in an institution, by the way, where he was getting picked on every single day of his life. The attendants there were rough on him, other kids beat him up. But it was the place that would keep him because they simply didn't care about their kids…or inmates, as they should have been called. Anyway, it was my holiday to spend with her, and I went grudgingly. Told my dad it was the last Christmas I'd spend in her house because I'd be eighteen shortly, and when I turned eighteen it was my intention never to see that woman again. So I went to her house. Of course, I was in my usual bad mood. Maybe even worse than usual, I don't know, because all I remember about what happened when I got there was that I locked myself in my room, and wondered why Robbie hated being locked in the way he did because it kept him away from her.

"So I was away in my own little world of anger and self-pity when my mother asked me to go and bring Robbie home for the holiday. I, of course, refused. And it didn't have anything to do with Robbie so much as it did me refusing to do what my mother asked. Besides, I knew Jack would go and get him. He was always the hero, the one

DIANNE DRAKE   251

who came through for Robbie no matter who else
let him down."

"But Jack's circumstances were different, Cade."

"Were they? He was being raised by my mother.
In fact, he lived under her brutality much longer
than I ever had to."

"Without expectations of her. She wasn't his
mother, and he knew that. Sure, it might have
been rough on him, having to claim her as his
mother, but maybe that was something he was
able to blot out. I mean, Jack seems a pretty un-
yielding kind of a guy, Cade. His sensibilities
probably weren't like yours, and—"

"You don't have to defend me, Belle. I was who
I was, justified or not. I loved Robbie, but I'm not
sure Robbie ever knew that because I was too
caught up in my own problems to ever reach out
to him the way I should have." Feelings he was
carrying over to Michael. Now she understood.
She was sending Michael away, the way Cade's
mother had sent Robbie away. Only the fine distinctions didn't matter, as Michael would have
come home in three weeks. Cade's guilt didn't
let him sort through the distinctions. All he saw
was that his son was getting sent away, and she

doubted Cade even knew that's why he'd come to Texas—to stop her. "So, what happened?"

"Jack got home late that night and said he'd go get Robbie the next day. Except no one ever told Robbie that was the plan. He expected to come home the day before, and when no one—when I didn't go to get him, he ran away. Afterwards, the authorities speculated he was trying to get home." He swiped angrily at a tear running down his cheek. "But I didn't have to speculate. I knew. Damn it, Belle, I knew!"

She was the one who drew in a ragged breath, trying to keep her balance, because all she could picture in her head was Michael out there lost and alone, somewhere, trying to get home. The same picture she knew was in Cade's head. Of Robbie. Even of Michael. "And?"

"December nights in Texas can get cold. That night it dipped down into the thirties, and Robbie wasn't dressed for it. Didn't even have on a pair of…" His voice cracked. "Shoes. The authorities found him two days later, but he was…" He shook his head. "The official cause of his death was exposure, but the death certificate might as well have said it was my anger that did him in, because if I'd gone to get him when he'd expected me, instead of hating my mother so much that I wouldn't do anything she asked…"

She scooted closer and took his hand. "I'm so sorry, Cade."

"Yeah, me, too," he said. "Fat lot of good that does Robbie, or even Michael."

But it did her good, because now she knew everything. And understood things in a way she'd never understood them before. Understood Cade in a way she'd never understood him before either. He'd spent a lifetime running away from himself, from his guilt. Spent all those years with his humanitarian causes, trying to make up for something he couldn't make right, not in himself, not in his world. It wasn't her he'd run from. Or marriage. Or Michael. All this time she'd thought it was, but it wasn't. "I, um…I don't know what it was like for you, having a mother like you described. I think it was terrible. Probably still is, because of the kinds of memories you still have. But you were a boy, Cade, and you deserved better. Even when Robbie died, you were still a boy— one who was left to carry guilt he didn't deserve."

"I never had enough time for him, Belle," he

said, his voice barely above a whisper. "Robbie didn't know what was going on with me. He was so innocent about the world, the way I see Michael sometimes, I doubt Robbie even knew that my mother despised him the way she did. All he knew was that he had two brothers, and one of them pushed him away." He turned to face her. "And look what I've done to Michael. I pushed you away, which pushed him away."

"You can't compare the two situations, Cade. You love Michael, and you're a good father."

"When, exactly, am I a good father?" he asked bitterly. "Tell me, because I sure as hell don't know."

"When you fly down here every other weekend to see him, even when you know that Michael hasn't yet become responsive to you, which has to hurt you more than anything I can imagine. And when we were back in Chicago and you were there, getting the same kind of response from him, yet you always came back when I'm sure it might have been easier to find reasons not to be so involved."

"And when I get here on my weekends, I'm jet-lagged, and he'd rather play video games. That's your definition of being a good father? Because to me it's just time. I'm spending time with Michael, but that's all."

"You're here now, and now is what counts."

"And he's lying unconscious in an intensive-care bed, and I'm not even able to—"

"To save your son?" she asked, giving in to the tears that had been trying to spill for a while now. "You're not even able to save our son?"

He twisted to face her, his tears as bitter as hers. "I don't know how to be enough for him, Belle. Or for you. I never did. All those years when I was growing up, I got good at shutting people out or running away when they got too close. Had lots of practice. Then you got in. But when it was just the two of us—you were strong. You got along fine in the world and I didn't feel as inadequate because of that. Then when Michael came along…"

"You were afraid to love us because you were afraid of failing us? Of failing Michael?" He'd run because he believed he'd failed Robbie and he was scared to death of failing Michael, too. "Did you know, Cade? Even before Michael was diagnosed with Asperger's syndrome, did you know what his diagnosis was going to be? Did you see something in him that made you think…? Did he remind you of Robbie?"

Slowly, very, very slowly, Cade withdrew his wallet then opened it. Inside was an old photo, one he kept behind his credit cards, library card and driver's license. One that didn't have its proper place in the plastic photo section where he carried photos of Michael. He withdrew that photo, and didn't look at it as he handed it over to Belle. "That's Robbie, close to the same age as Michael is now."

She held the photo for a moment before she looked down at it. And when she finally did… "They're identical," she whispered, as another round of tears splashed down her face. "Your brother and your son…" It was more than she could bear, more than Cade could bear as well, and as Belle clung to that photo, Cade pulled her into his arms, and the two of them sat underneath the Carolina jasmine with its yellow blooms, and Confederate jasmine with its white blooms, holding on to one another for dear life.

She loved this man. Had never stopped. But had never, truly known him the way she did now. More than loving him, she needed him and maybe this was the first time she'd ever realized she did. Maybe that's why it had been so easy for him to run in all the directions he had when they'd been married. She hadn't needed him enough to hold on to him when his need had been to run. Because she hadn't known him at all.

"I, um…" Jack said, stepping up to the trellis. "I wanted to be the one to tell you…" He cleared his throat. "Michael's…"

Cade and Belle split apart instantly, and she felt the knot form in her throat. The one that threatened to choke her even before Jack's words were out.

"I'm sorry, Belle, Cade. He's taken a turn for the worse. They've just put him on a ventilator."

CHAPTER EIGHT

"I MISS your voice, Michael." Belle wandered from the bed to the window, the way she'd done a thousand times before in the two days Michael had been on the ventilator, and like before she stared out, without really seeing anything. "When you wake up you're going to have to talk to me for a week straight without stopping so I can hear you again." He was stable, basically. The doctors kept telling her Jack's miracle drug was working. But all she could see, since an incident with respiratory distress two days earlier, was that he'd stayed the same. In limbo. A healing process, Amanda had said, and Jack had echoed that. Maybe so, but she was impatient, scared, frustrated. With all her skill, with all Cade's skill, they couldn't do anything for their son except be there. Talk. Reassure Michael. Reassure each other. And pray. "And we need to go get pizza. Do you know how long it's been since we've done that?" She was past the point of tears, at least for now. She was numb, though. Running on the fumes of empty energy. Going through the motions like she was a machine wound up to do what it was supposed to. Move from point A to point B, talk. Move from point B back to point A, talk.

She wanted her life back. All of it. She wanted Michael well and happy again, her medical practice thriving, and she wanted Cade. When she shut her eyes and pretended to see her life tomorrow, next week, next month, Cade was in it. But even that came with complications she didn't want to face as Cade would be going back to Chicago and she wouldn't. Or maybe she would go back with him. Right now, she didn't know. Couldn't plan.

And three more people were sick with *E. coli* in Big Badger. Jack had called in state investigators the previous day and, so far, they knew nothing more than she did. Later today the announcement would be made. The town would panic and blame her, and call her a deserter. Maybe destroy the cattle from the nearby ranches in reaction, maybe not. The rest of it was too horrible to think about.

"Last time we were in the hospital like this, I was getting ready to wrap you up and bring you home for the first time. I had this blue blanket for you—I'd bought a pink one and a blue one, so I'd be prepared either way. You were such a beautiful baby, Michael. You looked exactly like your daddy." And Robbie. Her heart ached for that tragedy as well. And it ached for the Cade she'd never known when they'd been married—the one who had loved too much, and too deeply, and carried guilt that wasn't his to carry. "And he was so nervous carrying you. He's a great surgeon, Michael. I don't know if you're even interested in medicine, but you could be great like your dad is, too. In anything you do." With all her heart, she believed that. And unlike Cade's mother, who had pushed her boys away and proved her hatred over and over, she would pull Michael close and help him achieve whatever his dream would be. Even bugs, if that's how it turned out.

"Anyway, here was this surgeon who saved lives every day, and his hands were shaking when he picked you up." A smile of reminiscence touched her lips. Shaking was an understatement. Cade had been a nervous wreck, reduced to a mass of quivering gelatin. His love for his son had been so clear. A love he had been afraid he would betray. "Eventually he managed to get you all the way out to the car, then he had to deal with getting you in the car seat, and..."

She'd been reciting story after story for two days now. They were her lifeline to Michael, and it was like if she stopped she'd lose that connection. "And he just stood there, not even sure where to begin. So I—"

The ventilator alarm suddenly sounded, and the rhythmic, mechanical breathing in and out seemed to strangle and fight against the very machine itself. Belle's heart clutched as she spun round, ready to run to the bed to save her son. But rather than springing into action, which was her automatic response as a doctor, as a mother she didn't move. Not one step. There was no need now, for, across the room, dwarfed in that mass of tubes and wires, Michael was watching her, wide-eyed. Bright, wide eyes. Except he really wasn't watching her so much as he was studying all the machines to which he was hooked up. Analyzing them, trying to figure out the way they worked, the way only Michael would do.

"Welcome back," Belle said, fighting for calm as she grabbed hold of the window ledge for support. Then she pulled her phone from her pocket and texted Cade, who was on his way back from Big Badger with fresh clothes. Her text was simple. Two words. *He's awake.* The two most beautiful words she'd ever texted in her life. "So now, Michael, let me explain to you what all these machines are for." That might have been an odd statement from most mothers, and most mothers might have been crying and throwing themselves all over their sons, but this mother knew her son and her son would want to know every last aspect of every last machine. So Belle kissed him on the head, then began her explanation of the EKG machine, and what the tracing going across its screen meant.

Cade's breath caught in his throat when the jingle indicating he had a text message sounded. It was the jingle he'd set specifically for Belle—Mozart's "Eine Kleine Nachtmusik." A simple piece of music he knew she hated, while she thought he thought she loved it. This time, though, it frightened him as they'd promised to call or text only if it was an emergency. Otherwise they would keep the line open just in case. Since that moment in the garden when he'd told her everything, they'd barely spoken. There really wasn't much to say right now anyway, and he was hoping the lack of words had no significance, while fearing that the lack was more significant than he wanted to know.

For now, he didn't know, though. Didn't want to think about it, dwell on it, wonder about it either. But the jingle of his text message… Rather than looking at it, he pulled off to the side of the road and held his phone between his shaking hands for a full minute, only staring at the icon indicating he had a message, thinking of all the ways his life could be after he read it. Finally, the curdled dread of not knowing forced him to tap that icon, then the message appeared. *He's awake.*

Cade slumped back in his seat, closed his eyes, and let the tears flow. His son was awake. Life just got good again.

"What comes next?" Cade asked, standing in the hospital hallway, looking through the window at Michael. He had been extubated now, meaning no breathing tube, no ventilator. In fact, most of the monitors had been discontinued, and Michael had protested when they'd been rolled out of the room because he liked them, liked the way they functioned. So typical. Probably in a day knew as much about their functioning as the hospital biomedical equipment tech did.

Belle stepped up behind him, stood so close she could smell a hint of lime in his aftershave. "They're moving him into the pediatric ward tomorrow, and if all goes well, we can take him home in a couple of days." She wanted to lean her head on his shoulder or slip her hand into his, feel his strength, feel anything from Cade, but he was so shut off again. "After that, a normal recovery, I'm hoping. He said he wants to go camping, though. He's already told me that he wants to go every weekend for the rest of the summer."

Just the three of them. "Me, you, and Dad," he'd told her, then added, "Uncle Jack should come, too." A simple, beautiful wish she wanted to make happen, but didn't know if she could.

"Too bad life isn't that uncomplicated," Cade said, on a sigh. He turned to face her. "Look, I've been giving this a lot of thought. I think it's time for me to go back to Chicago. Not now, specifically, but after he's up and about. And I've also been thinking that maybe I should reduce my time with him since my coming and going disrupts his routine. I don't want to do that to him. Also, because of his health right now, Michael's not going to be able to go with me to Chicago later on this summer like we'd planned, and since I don't want to break up his life any more than it's already been broken up, I'm thinking that I should cancel seeing him during those weeks altogether, and let him get back to the life he counts on. But I'm not running away, Belle. I want you to know that. I'm just trying to let Michael have what he needs most."

"And what he needs most isn't you?" Cade was leaving? Michael was out of danger and no matter what he called it, or whatever he believed was his reason, Cade was running away? This couldn't be happening, not when she'd started letting herself think that—well, maybe they had a future. But no. Cade was going to do what Cade wanted to do. Like always. "You don't want to disrupt his life?" she added, trying to keep her emotions level when everything inside her was about to boil over. "So now, when he's going to need you more than he ever has in his life, you're going to just leave him? I don't get it, Cade. Why would you do something like that?"

"Because he needs you, Belle. You're his stability. Not me. I'm the one who wanders in every now and then and changes his life for a little while. But Michael needs the consistency of his real life back, and I'm not part of that."

"Because you don't want to be part of it! When they extubated him, do you know the first thing he said to me?" She didn't wait for his response before she answered, "He asked where you were. He wanted you, Cade. You! And you're going to walk away from that?" She shook her head violently. "This isn't about Robbie, isn't about the guilt you feel over his tragedy. I'm so sorry about that, and I don't know what it's going to take to convince you it wasn't your fault. But that's not what this is about, Cade. It's about your son. You love him, and you told me you'd come here because you wanted to establish your relationship with him. Yet when that's starting to happen, you're talking about turning your back on him."

"Not turning my back on him, Belle. Just letting him get his life back the way it should be. That's all."

"You know what, Cade? If you can't be here the way Michael expects you to be, the way I expect you to be, I'm not sure I want you here at all. So maybe you should go back to Chicago now, today. Right this very minute." They were harsh words she knew she would regret later on, but they spilled out anyway. "Because you do disrupt his life. It takes him a full day to get used to you being here, then another day after you've left to get over the sadness he feels when you go. What are you going to do about that? And what are you going to do about the way I feel? Because I'm involved in this, too, and I go through that same sadness. Sometimes when you go back to Chicago, I ache so much I can barely breathe, barely function. And I look forward to your next visit, even though most of the time we barely speak. Even so, I've lived for those moments, Cade. Never dated anyone, never wanted to, because every other week I got to see you for a minute or two. And no one else ever came close to being...you." Bad, good, in between, Cade had always been the only one. "But I can't keep doing that, can't let you do it to me. Or to Michael. So leave. Get out of here.

Leave us alone, and we'll adjust just fine without you!"

"But you've never let me in, Belle. Not into your life with Michael. This is where I've always been." He pointed to the spot in which he was standing. "Right here in the hall, gazing through the window at what I didn't have, couldn't have."

"Because that's where you wanted to be." She looked in at Michael, who was watching them. The expression on his face was unreadable, something caught between sadness and bewilderment, and one that broke her heart for reasons she didn't understand. "I understand now why you did what you did but, Cade, it wasn't me. You're the one who never let me in. So telling me I never let you in…maybe that's the convenient excuse, the one that's easier for you to deal with, but I always wanted you to be part of the family. Wanted you to spend more time with Michael. And more than anything else, I wanted more time with you, but there never seemed to be enough of it, and you were always someplace else. You were doing good things, setting up clinics in areas without medical help, volunteering as a surgeon with your visiting doctors' group. Even though I didn't understand why you were doing it, how could I say something, or even ask you not to go, when you were involved in such great causes?

"Because if I had, I'd have looked…selfish, or petty. Yet I couldn't compete with all those things you did, Cade. Sometimes, though, I was so…lonely. I'd wake up in the morning and ache to have you there next to me, but you weren't. And it was like I had this hole in my heart. One that always reminded me that I wasn't enough to keep you home. So maybe I did overcompensate by smothering Michael more than I should, and maybe it looked to you like I was shutting you out, but you were the one closing the doors, and I didn't know what to do about it because you never told me why. Maybe, if you'd let me in, or told me why you were keeping me out, we could have figured out what to do to help you. I'm not holding it against you, Cade, because I don't know what I'd have done if I'd been carrying the kind of guilt you've been carrying all these years. But you should have trusted me. If you loved me enough to marry me, you should have trusted me."

She looked in at Michael again, who was studying them now through the lens of his camera. "He loves that thing, you know. The second thing he said after they yanked the breathing tube was that he wanted his camera, and I have an idea that everything in his room has been photographed from every angle a dozen times."

"Robbie did, too. I gave him a camera for his eighth birthday...not even a digital one, but one that used film. And he took pictures..." A smile crept to Cade's face. "Mostly of bugs. His world was a lot simpler than Michael's but he loved his bugs. Anyway, he had scrapbooks full of pictures, and he could spend hours looking at them. Didn't know their names the way Michael does, didn't even care. He just liked looking at them. The hell of it was, he couldn't find his way home if he wandered out of the front yard, but if he encountered a bug while he was lost, he could describe it in such amazing ways." He shut his eyes, sighed heavily. "I never meant to hurt you, Belle. But the whole responsibility thing...you did it better than I did. My strong suit was running away. Keeping my distance. And I knew it was wrong, but I didn't know how to stop it."

"Does it bother you that Michael looks so much like your brother?"

"What bothers me is that because of my circumstances I couldn't be the brother Robbie needed me to be. I was so caught up in myself, in my own pain—"

"You were a child, Cade. You can apply adult sensibilities to your situation now, but back then you were simply a child."

"So was Robbie. So is Michael. And I can't be the father he needs me to be."

"Because you couldn't be the brother Robbie needed you to be? Is that why you're still running?" she asked gently. "Because you're afraid you'll let Michael down the way you think you let your brother down?"

"Well, that seems to be my history, doesn't it? One way or another, I've let down everybody I've ever cared for. All my good intentions are outweighed by my deeds."

"Which is why you want to start running again, isn't it, Cade? Why you want to quit seeing Michael as often, for his own good? Or is it for your own good, because you're scared to death that something you do will bring on another tragedy like what happened to your brother?"

"What he doesn't need is disruption, and that's

all I am to him. You've said it. I've seen it. I'm nothing more than a great big disruption, and I love Michael too much to do that to him."

She laid a gentle hand on his arm. "So why is he taking your picture right now, if that's all you are to him? Because he's been clicking away, nonstop, for the past several minutes."

Cade turned to look in the window. Smiled, then waved at Michael. "What am I supposed to do, Belle?" he asked. "Tell me. Make a suggestion. Give me a solution. Anything."

"Be his father. Love him the way you do and simply be his father." She slipped her arm around his waist. "He's not Robbie, Cade. He's Michael, and he needs you. I'm not promising it's going to be easy. Not even promising that he'll be very responsive. But he needs you to be his dad, and you need to be his dad."

He spun to face her. "That's all you want from me? Or expect from me? Because here's the thing. Probably the most honest thing you've ever heard from me. If I were to do what I wanted, nobody's feelings or needs considered other than my own, I would move here, live in Big Badger if that's what I had to do to be Michael's father. The problem in that, though, is you live there, and I can't spend the rest of my life seeing you every day, knowing what I lost, knowing I can't get it back. Because I want it back, Belle. All of it. You, Michael, our life—the one I took away from us. I want everything that was good, and that's the real reason I came to Texas in the first place. To see if there was any hope left for us." He shrugged. "But all I see are the ways I've failed you everywhere I look. Even now, that expression on your face—"

"That expression?" she said, her voice barely above a whisper. "Do you know what that expression is, Cade? It's me, telling you I've never not wanted to be a family—the three of us, maybe even four or five of us. Not only Michael and me, but Michael and me and…you."

From his hospital bed, Michael aimed and shot, once, twice, a dozen times. Then he tucked his camera under the covers, smiled, and dozed off.

"I've got a lead on about five different things it could be," Jack said. He handed Cade's laptop computer over to Michael, who was out of Intensive Care now, and was turning his hospital room into his own private home away from home.

"I've done every test possible, read the results so many times I've memorized them, cultured things no one would ever culture for *E. coli*, and the good news is nothing is pointing to contaminants in the groundwater. In other words, as far as I can tell, it's not related to the cattle. But the people in Big Badger are pushing for an answer. So far they haven't done anything more than ask questions, which is probably the most encouraging news I can give you right now. Unfortunately, since you and Cade have been busy here, we've had another four cases diagnosed."

Belle slumped back in her chair. "It feels like I've been away from there a million years." She glanced at Cade, who was propped up in bed alongside Michael, getting ready to help him download his photos into the laptop. "I think I need to get back. So since Michael may be released day after tomorrow..." She looked at Cade. "Do you think you could handle it here, if I went home for the day?"

Both Michael and Cade waved her off. "We'll be fine," Cade said, then winked.

"Fine," Michael mimicked, without the wink.

She turned her attention to Jack. "I get the feeling they don't need me."

"I'm the one who needs you. Between trying to manage your medical practice, and that includes going out to the ranches as well as doing my investigations…" He shook his head. "All I have to say about it is, hop into my car, Dr. Carter, and I'll be more than happy to take you home and turn your medical practice back over to you."

"Are you coming back?" Michael asked.

"Tomorrow some time. Not sure when, exactly, but I'll be back. Why? Do you want me to bring you something?" Any number of his gadgets and books came to mind.

"Can you bring me my strawberry jam?"

Belle frowned for a moment. "We don't have any strawberry jam, but I can stop at the grocery and buy some, if you want it." It was an odd request, as she didn't recall having had strawberry jam in her pantry in a long, long time. Probably not since they'd lived in Chicago. But she was so relieved that Michael was on the mend and getting his appetite back as well, she'd have promised him almost anything. "Do you want peanut butter to go with it?"

He shook his head. "Bread and jam. That's all."

Again, another odd request. "Then I'll buy you some jam."

"Not at the store. Mrs. Ellison makes it and everybody buys it from her."

Jack immediately became alert. "Well, I'll be damned," he said, pulling his cellphone from his pocket. "Home-made strawberry jam!"

"Do you think that could be the cause?" Belle asked, totally stunned. She'd set herself up to expect big things, and this was so small. Something she'd have never suspected in a million years, yet Jack knew, or at least suspected, and if the jam turned out to be the cause, she owed him for this one, and she only hoped he would stay around for a while so she could find a way to repay him. Maybe help him find a way back to his brother? Or spend time with Michael? "How could that be?"

"Contaminated strawberries, most likely." He looked at Michael. "What kind of jam is it?" he asked. "The kind she gets out of a cupboard or the kind she gets out of the freezer?"

"The freezer," Michael replied, looking annoyed at being interrupted.

"Uncooked strawberries…contaminated uncooked strawberries. I read about it happening up in Oregon once."

"Which is why the outbreak was limited," Cade said. "Remember, you'd mentioned it to me, wondered why only certain people were getting sick? So now we have the answer—they were Virginia's customers."

Jack clicked a number into his cellphone, then a few seconds later said to the health authority on the other end, "It's probably the freezer jam being sold by a local woman by the name of Virginia Ellison. We need to put out the alert, recall all the jam, check the strawberry supply source…"

"I think you solved it, Michael," Cade said, smiling at Belle.

Michael didn't respond, though. He was too busy putting together a slideshow of his photos. Soon, very soon, he had plans for it. Right now those plans were clicking away in his speedy little brain and nothing else mattered.

"Four days, no new cases," Belle said. She was stretched out on her exam table, head on the pillow, legs over the end, staring up at the ceiling.

Life was getting back to normal, and today she'd seen three Big Badger men. Maybe, just maybe, she was making headway in that. "Maudie's on the mend, Jack's enjoying taking care of Michael while we're working. I'd say all is well here. And when Michael's up to it, I promised him another camping trip out on the creek at the Ruda del Monte. Maybe Jack will stay around for a while and go with us—I'm assuming you're going, too."

"I expect I'll have to since I own it. Not the whole ranch. Just those few acres."

"What?" she said, bolting straight up. "You bought it?"

Tossing his white coat over one of the chairs, he walked over to the table and stood at the end of it, taking his place between her knees, looking Belle straight in the eyes. "When you said you wanted to be a family of three, or four, or five, I took that literally. And since that can't happen if I'm in Chicago, I decided to see if that little patch of land came with a price tag. It did, and I'll be talking with an architect in a couple of weeks. Something about a sprawling ranch house up on the knoll overlooking the creek."

"Cade, I—I don't know what to say. The other

day, when we were talking, it was all the emotion of the moment. People say things, do things they wouldn't normally do, when they're under stress."

"Like arguing me out of walking away?"

"That was real. I don't want you leaving Michael. He needs you, and he's finally warming up to you."

"What about you, Belle?" he asked, leaning over and rubbing his hands up her legs, from her ankles to her knees. "Tell me what's best for Belle, not Michael, since we both already know what's best for Michael."

She chilled to his touch, and it was such a simple touch. But she always had. "It would be easy to say we should get back together for Michael, but that's not what I want, Cade. Michael has both of us, no matter how we work this out."

"So, what wouldn't be so easy to say?"

"That I want to do this for—for me. The purely selfish me who likes it when you touch me, or wink at me, or smile at me. And I want it for us, too. But it scares me like nothing's ever scared me in my life, because I know what it's like to lose you, and I can't do that again. It hurt too much the first time."

"I never thought I could be good enough for him. I couldn't for Robbie, then after Michael was diagnosed, it was easy to step back because you swooped in and smothered him. Maybe I should have fought harder to stay closer, but when I looked at our beautiful little boy, then thought about what I'd done, or hadn't done for another beautiful little boy, I always knew Michael would be fine with you. You're strong. And fierce."

"But so are you. And Michael needs that strength and fierceness from both of us. It's going to be a difficult world out there for him. Sometimes it scares me, thinking of all the things he's going to have to face. I mean, our child has Asperger's syndrome, Cade. For me, it's simply the way he is. It's normal, he's normal. But that's naive, because I know how people react, and some of them are going to make it tough on our little boy. They won't see Michael first, they'll see his diagnosis. So I've overcompensated because..."

"Because you're a good mother. It took me a while to get where I needed to be, Belle, but I've grown up, and I want to be as good a father as you are a mother. More than that, I want to be a good husband."

"But can you make it here in Texas? I know you bought that land because that's what I want. If you practice medicine in Big Badger, though, it's going to be general medicine. Can you do that?"

"Because it's for my family, for a while."

"You can only stay for a while?" she asked, feeling her gut clench into a knot. "Then what?"

"Then I'll be a surgeon again. Maybe not on a large scale like I am now, but even a small-town hospital needs a surgeon on call."

"A hospital? What hospital?"

"Actually, I'm thinking it will be more like a clinic with extended services for now. Something that will grow in the future, though. Michael's already agreed to do the computers for us, by the way. He told me he's getting better at networking, and that he has some ideas to maximize our efficiency."

"You asked your son before you asked me?" she said, scooting toward the end of the exam table. "He's seven, Cade. Don't you think we should wait until he's at least eight before we turn our hospital's computers over to him?"

Cade chuckled. "If we can keep him contained that long. He's already doing some preliminary designs, and they involve games in the children's ward. They also involve Jack."

"How?"

Cade shrugged. "Not sure, really. But Jack's looking for a place to rent. Said he's got to make up for lost time with his nephew. He really loves Michael, you know. The way he loved Robbie."

"How will you do, having him around?"

"We're OK. Not great, but good enough. Tolerant. We've got a way to go, but he's going to be here for a while, so who knows what's going to happen?"

"Will he be working as a doctor?"

"He didn't say. I suppose that's something he'll have to work out on his own, in time."

Belle scooted all the way to the end of the exam table, locking her knees around Cade's waist and wrapping her arms around his neck. "Well, I've got something I want to work out right now. And this time I'm holding on," she said. "Never letting go."

"This time I'm holding you to that promise." He gave her a quick kiss on the lips, then stepped back, a delicious twinkle coming to his eyes. "We don't have any more patients scheduled in this afternoon, do we?"

In answer, Belle undid the top button of her blouse. "Actually, Doctor, you do have one more patient to see. She has an incurable condition, I'm afraid. One she needs you to check out." Another two buttons came undone. "And I think you should probably lock the door before you begin your exam, then come and listen to her heart because I think you'll like what you're going to hear."

"What am I going to hear?" he asked, putting his stethoscope in his ears, and placing the bell to Belle's heart. He listened for a moment, then smiled. "I love you, too, Belle. With all my heart."

"All my heart," she whispered back

"It's done," Michael said, hitting a few buttons on the laptop and pulling up a banner, "Michael's Slideshow."

OK, maybe it wasn't the most imaginative title, but Belle was bursting with pride. These last weeks had been rough in some spots, good in others. Overall, though, it took both the bad and good to get them to this place, and this was where she wanted to stay, forever. "Bet it's got lots of bugs in it," she said, settling down on the couch next to Michael, pulling her feet up under her, while Cade sat on the other side of him, kicking off his shoes and making himself family-style comfortable.

"No bugs," Michael said, quite seriously. Then quickly changed his mind. "Well, maybe a few."

"Bugs are good," Cade responded, giving his son the thumbs up. "So…" He faked a drumroll on the table in front of the couch. "Let's see it."

Michael hit the play button, and sure enough, bugs. But not the bugs they'd expected. The first several shots were of Belle's dubious reaction to various bugs when they'd gone camping at the Ruda del Monte, including a couple of notorious screams, a few well-placed gasps, and one particularly funny shot of her running away from a moth. Then there were pictures of Cade watching Belle respond to the bugs. Lots of those, actually. And shots of the two of them together, at times arguing, at times frowning, at times smiling. Through Michael's eyes they saw stress, pain, fear…they saw happiness, joy, distance, and separation. It was a mural of a family's struggles, their feelings, their triumphs and defeats, and Belle was stunned. "It's beautiful, Michael," she whispered.

So real and so…honest. It's what Michael saw when he looked at them.

"It's you and Dad," he said, more interested in the various ways he could adjust his slideshow. Faster, slower, at times on its side, it all said the same thing. This was how they were, through Michael's eyes. What he saw was the struggle, and the progress. Most of all, he saw the love. And the last photos, of their embrace in the hall outside his intensive-care window, that's the one that said it all. The one that said they were a family again. Well, until a succession of beetles, caterpillars, and grasshoppers crossed the screen. And, at the very end, a moth. Michael looked at his dad, and asked, "Think she'll scream?"

Cade smiled at Belle as Michael hopped up off the couch, finished with all the family togetherness, and scampered to the front porch to wait for his uncle, who'd promised to take him on the bug hunt of his life.

"Will you scream?" Cade asked.

"Could we cuddle instead?" Which was what they did.

Minutes later, looking inside from the porch, Michael aimed his camera and shot a photo of his parents. Then reviewed it and smiled. Tomorrow he'd take out the moth and put this one in instead. "The end," he said resolutely, as Jack came up the steps to get him.

"The beginning," Jack responded, looking in the window at Cade and Belle. "I think, Michael, that this is only the beginning."

* * * * *

Mills & Boon® Large Print Medical

December

January

February

Mills & Boon® Large Print Medical

March

HER MOTHERHOOD WISH	Anne Fraser
A BOND BETWEEN STRANGERS	Scarlet Wilson
ONCE A PLAYBOY...	Kate Hardy
CHALLENGING THE NURSE'S RULES	Janice Lynn
THE SHEIKH AND THE SURROGATE MUM	Meredith Webber
TAMED BY HER BROODING BOSS	Joanna Neil

April

A SOCIALITE'S CHRISTMAS WISH	Lucy Clark
REDEEMING DR RICCARDI	Leah Martyn
THE FAMILY WHO MADE HIM WHOLE	Jennifer Taylor
THE DOCTOR MEETS HER MATCH	Annie Claydon
THE DOCTOR'S LOST-AND-FOUND HEART	Dianne Drake
THE MAN WHO WOULDN'T MARRY	Tina Beckett

May

MAYBE THIS CHRISTMAS...?	Alison Roberts
A DOCTOR, A FLING & A WEDDING RING	Fiona McArthur
DR CHANDLER'S SLEEPING BEAUTY	Melanie Milburne
HER CHRISTMAS EVE DIAMOND	Scarlet Wilson
NEWBORN BABY FOR CHRISTMAS	Fiona Lowe
THE WAR HERO'S LOCKED-AWAY HEART	Louisa George